WHOEVER HAS THE HEART

WHOEVER HAS THE HEART

Jennie Melville

St. Martin's Press
New York

Library of Congress Cataloging-in-Publication Data

Melville, Jennie.
    Whoever has the heart / Jennie Melville.
        p.   cm.
    "A Thomas Dunne book."
    ISBN 0-312-11099-5 (hardcover)
    1. Daniels, Charmian (Fictitious character)—Fiction.
    2. Policewomen—England—Fiction.   I. Title.
    PR6063.E44W45   1994
    823'.914—dc20   94-417
                                                                           CIP

First published in Great Britain by Macmillan London Limited.

First U.S. Edition: June 1994
10 9 8 7 6 5 4 3 2 1

'By tradition, whoever has the heart gets the rest of the body.'
Unnatural Death, Michael Baden M.D. with Judith Adler Hennrssee

ONE

The small house was in a state of polite but decided disarray, like an elderly lady of breeding who had lost her way and wanted to find it again. The house stood back from the village street with a few modest flower-beds in front and a walled garden set against the grounds of the manor house behind. Across the way was the church with its squat Norman tower and well-filled graveyard.

Yesterday I had watched a man fall apart, and bloodily die. That was yesterday, the house was today.

I stood looking over the wall into the garden, just as run-down as the house with more weeds and rank grass than flowers, but you could see a desperate pansy fighting upwards. I felt like that pansy.

Nice house. I couldn't afford it, I shouldn't have it, but I wanted it desperately.

I meant to have it.

I went back to the village pub where my friend Mary Erskine was drinking gin and tonic by the leaping wood fire.

'The roof looks a bit dodgy,' I said. 'And where can I park the car?'

'Have a drink.' A glass of dry sherry appeared as if by magic. Bill the barman at the Red Dragon was, needless to say, a friend and admirer of Mary Erskine. Some of the magic brushed off on me. 'There's a lane at the back, you have an entrance to a garage.'

1

I supposed she meant the kind of shed I had observed. 'How long's it been empty?'

'About nine months, but Aunt Bea neglected it for years. She couldn't get about, you see. It's not as bad inside as you might think.'

'I haven't seen that yet.'

'And she left some very nice rugs around that you could buy. I believe there's a Flemish tapestry on one wall too.' She saw the surprise on my face. I didn't move in a world which hung tapestry on the wall. Policewomen don't. 'She did live in a castle at one time, you know. Castle Derelict it may have been but it was genuine, like the tapestry.' Mary Erskine gave a little giggle. 'She had it up there to hide the damp.'

'Thanks for telling me.'

'You'd smell it as soon as you went in . . . Want the key?' She pulled it out of her pocket, a great black object, which looked as old as the house.

Mrs Armitage had died almost a year ago, or so I had been told. I wasn't clear if Lady Mary had been left the house in her aunt's will, but she seemed to be in charge of it. If anyone was.

'How did you get the key?'

'I've had it for years. Aunt Bea gave it to me. I used to call about once a week when she was immobile. She died in her sleep, more or less, sitting up in a chair in the kitchen. Not a bad way to go. Small stroke, the doctor said, he'd been looking after her for weeks.' Mary swigged some more gin and took a deep breath. 'I miss the old lady more than I can say. She kept me on an even keel.'

Then she had a job, I thought. Mary Dalmeny Erskine was the charming, feckless, impecunious daughter to an aristocratic family of some lineage and no money. She had a house not far from where I lived in the royal borough of Windsor. Lately, I had felt that I had been handed over the job vacated by Aunt Bea.

2

'When did she die?'

'Just under a year ago. She's buried in the churchyard, beneath the yew tree, across the road from the house. She said she wanted to be in sight of the house and near the pub.'

That told me something about Beatrice Armitage.

I took the key and let myself into the house. It did not smell of damp, as Mary Erskine had said, but of old furniture and dust. An open window or two would remedy that, I thought.

A room on either side of the front door, a hall running through to the back where a narrow staircase curved upwards in simple elegance. The tapestry covered this wall. It was dark and in bad repair but I could make out a female warrior in a breastplate and a helmet with a lion by her side. She was standing in a wood; small animals peered around the trees. A squirrel, a hare, a startled deer, and a white hound. No doubt it was Flemish, I had seen something in that style in the Louvre in Paris.

There were indeed some rugs on the floors, and they might be valuable if cleaned. There was no furniture, all had been sold, and only its ghostly presence remained in the scent of lavender and beeswax. But in the kitchen was the oldest refrigerator that I had ever seen. It was so old that it could even be new art, since most of its workings were on its outside, like the Pompidou Centre in Paris or the subject of some operation who had had all his organs arranged on his head. There was also a great black stove that looked as though it ate coal.

Upstairs were three empty rooms and a surprisingly comfortable-looking bathroom. Above were attics. I climbed the very narrow stairs but found the attic door locked. Disappointed, I went back downstairs and sat on the window seat looking out on the flower garden, which was overgrown and neglected like all else.

Yet the room felt comfortable. The house was run-down, in need of all sorts of repair, but it was a happy

3

house. Generations of people had lived here and had liked their home. Like a child or an animal that had always been well treated, it had responded.

I needed that house. And the house needed me.

Houses may not live in the way animals do, but they can certainly die, and this little house was very near to death. If someone did not repair the roof and attend to the stonework it would die. Rot would come creeping down from the roof and up from the cellars (was there a cellar? Bound to be in a house of this age) and some developer would knock it down and run up a clump of hideous new houses.

The sun came in through the window and warmed my back, a winter sun, but there was heat in it. The light showed up the dust on the floor and on the paintwork. There had been a lot of furniture in the room once, I could see the marks on the walls. A big cabinet or book-case over there, a looking-glass above the fire, and many pictures. All gone.

I took a piece of paper out of my pocket and started to work out figures. What I would need, how much I would have to borrow.

It was an envelope with my name and address on it: Charmian Daniels, Maid of Honour Row, Windsor.

I would keep on that small establishment, I was required to live in Windsor, but I was too close to my job there and I needed a distance. For over two years now, I had been head of SRADIC: Southern Register, Documentation and Index of Crime. I co-ordinated all the records of crime for all the southern Forces, not including London, but the Met had an obligation to liaise with me. My unit was based in Windsor, with a sub-office in Slough. I had also recently been given the go-ahead to set up my own small investigating unit, for already it was clear that there were going to be occasions when I would want to initiate my own independent enquiries. I had certain other more secret duties which I did not talk about. I was a high-ranking police officer and a powerful lady.

It went without saying that I was also, on occasion, an overworked and anxious one. As they say: it went with the territory. I had friends and allies but I also had enemies. I wanted space away from them all.

I also had a lover. Humphrey Kent, a powerful figure in his own right. I needed space from him as well.

I got up and paced the room: it was a good size. I had been on my own too long now to be able to join up easily with another person. Humphrey had his own house in Windsor and an inherited country place, very lovely, rather grand in its own way. If we married, these would be my homes.

But I wanted my own base. Meant to have it, said a voice inside me.

We would marry, we both desired it, I could see it coming quite soon, but I was not a sharer. I might have to give up Maid of Honour Row, I could see that coming too, but this house I would have.

Besides, there was something in my bones that ached for this house. I felt as though it would pick up my past and knit it to my future, making everything a whole. My life had been fragmented by various things, like death, and ambition.

I walked back to the pub where Mary Erskine was sitting by the fire, her eyes closed, her face looked pinched and tired. I knew well that she brought her troubles on her own head, and sometimes involved me in them, but I always forgave her.

'Is there a cellar?' I asked.

She opened her eyes. 'Yes, but you have to go outside to go down to it.'

'Inconvenient.'

'I think when the house was built the manservant used to sleep down there.'

'Was the house big enough for a manservant?'

She yawned. 'Oh, yes, girls up in the attic, and the men outside. A primitive form of birth control. Not that it always worked.'

I sat down beside her. 'I shall buy it.'

'Oh, good. I like to think of you having it.'

'If the price is right.' The mortgage might be tricky to arrange.

'You old Scot. I shall see it is. The best thing that's happened all week, bringing you here.' There was real feeling in her voice.

I laughed but not unkindly, I could afford to show sympathy. 'What's up? I can see something is.'

'Just parted for ever with my best young man.' She stood up. 'Oh, what the hell, he's a soldier without a penny and I haven't got anything.'

'You've done that before and he's always come back.' I liked her young man.

'No, this time it's for good.'

'Is money so important?'

'You can't get married on minus nothing. I can't take my debts into the marriage bed.'

I looked at her thoughtfully. Lack of money had never so far stopped my lady doing anything she wanted. And wasn't all this talk about the marriage bed a bit archaic? They'd probably been in and out of bed countless times already. There must be something else.

But aristocrats like Mary could go archaic on you at times, you never could be sure when you would scratch the skin off a scab that really mattered. I felt quite smug: a graduate of a Scottish university, brought up in a more egalitarian world, had no need to keep class rules.

Mary gave the fire a vicious poke.

'You're not doing the fire any good.'

She put the poker down. 'Actually, he's chucked me.' She saw my questioning look. 'He found out that Billy Damiani asked me to go to the Ritz in Paris with him.'

'And you went? You are a fool, Mary.'

6

'It's known as being my own worst enemy,' she said dolefully.

'He's a snake, that man.'

'He has great charm,' said Mary. 'And of course, he's enormously rich.'

'I'd like to know where he got that name from. And I wish I knew where they came from.' He had a sister whom one saw around. 'I'll try to find out. He might be worth study.'

'You wouldn't!' She was shocked, in her world one did not investigate a chum. Not even a risky one like Billy Damiani.

'Why not?'

'Not today, please. He's coming over to give us lunch, the food's frightfully good here.' She added, 'And very expensive.'

I stood up. 'Count me out. I'll get a sandwich.'

'But he specially wants to meet you.'

'He has met me.'

'Not properly.'

'You set this up,' I said. 'I'm really angry.' I think I was.

Lady Mary smiled. 'Oh, go and walk it off.'

I walked out and was preparing to bang the door behind me when the childishness of this struck me, and I slowed down.

'Come back just before one o'clock,' Mary called after me. 'We'll settle the business about Bea's house before he gets here, Billy's always late.' She took a step towards me, looking for something from me of understanding and sympathy. 'I do love my soldier boy.'

Funny way of showing it, I thought, but I was not shocked or even surprised. Mary Dalmeny Erskine's code of behaviour was not mine but I accepted it as part of her world. Tough on the soldier boy, who obviously felt plain sexual jealousy, and who could blame him? Still, years in the police had taught me something about the range of human behaviour.

7

I walked down the village, turning towards the church. I had already visited Brideswell several times before so I knew the layout. It was a remarkably beautiful village, set in a wooded valley through which ran a narrow, rushing river. As a village it was unusually complete, it still had a school, a post office, and a baker's shop. Needless to say all were under threat as uneconomic but had survived because most of the village was part of the estate of the family that owned the manor. There was a butcher but fish came round in a van once a week. If I bought Muff here for a visit then I would have to consider the fish supply.

The main street was narrow with the houses facing each other very closely, although Mrs Beatrice Armitage's house was set back from the road behind its slip of front garden.

I saw the parson hurry down the path from the church and leap on to his motorbike. He was responsible for two other parishes so he was a busy man. A bachelor, a theologian on his way up to a bishopric, he gave me a wave as he passed. He was gone before I could wave back. I walked through the lich-gate into the churchyard. A weatherbeaten board informed me that I was approaching the church of St Edwin the Martyr in the parish of Brideswell; The Rector: the Reverend Thomas Baxter, MA. Churchwardens: Ermine Sprott and Jack Bean. I dragged my coat closer around me, the usual chill March wind was blowing, damp and with a hint of snow.

In this part of the churchyard the graves were immemorially old, the inscriptions eroded by age, and some had disappeared completely, but nearer to the road all the graves were newer. I could see a man putting flowers on one of these graves.

There was the yew tree, dark and sturdy. I walked towards it thinking that Mrs Armitage had chosen her burial site well.

I had no difficulty in finding her grave since Aunt Bea

lay in solitary state underneath the yew, but the tomb itself was plain enough, still starkly new. She had been dead only nine months, but the stone was even newer.

Beatrice Alice Armitage, widow of Lt. Colonel Earnsly Armitage
Widow also of the Earl Finden of Ladlaw in Ross
And of le Duc de Caze de La Tour.

Quite a woman, I thought. She had moved in several different worlds before dying in this quiet Berkshire village. I bent down and put my hand on the marble. 'You might see me in your house, Mrs Armitage, if you can look across.' Some needles from the yew were spattered across the stone and I brushed them gently aside.

I stood up and walked towards the other graves, lined up in neat rows. The man with the flowers was standing watching me. I suppose strangers were rare in the village.

My gaze was attracted to three graves, side by side, plain white stones with a small angel sitting on each; except for this decoration they looked stark and uncompromising.

A husband, wife, and daughter were buried here. Arthur, Hilda, and Angela Beasley. They had been buried within the last year and they had died within a few days of each other.

An accident, I decided. Car crash or a fire at home.

The man of the flowers was approaching me. He was tall and thin, about forty, wearing dark tweeds. His face was tanned as if he spent a lot of time in the open air. He was hard to place, he could have been a farmer or a poet.

'Quite a death rate in this village,' I said absently.

'Oh, them.' He shrugged, but offered no information.

'Was it an accident?'

'Illness of some sort,' he said. 'Visiting, are you?' I nodded. 'Visiting friends?'

'Just visiting.'

9

'Saw you looking at the Duchess's grave.'

'Mrs Armitage? Didn't call herself Duchess, did she?' Not claiming a title after remarriage was one of the social rules Lady Mary's class did keep. Liberal about sex, strict about titles, that was how it went.

'Did when she felt like it.'

So Beatrice Armitage called herself what she fancied, as she fancied. I thought she might have done it as a joke and guessed I would have liked her.

'Thinking of taking her house?'

Was nothing secret here?

'Saw you going into it.'

'I have looked at it.'

He touched his cap and started to move away. 'Shouldn't come here, if I were you. Like you said: high death rate.'

I stood where I was till he had gone, and then I walked across the path to the grave with the flowers where a spring posy of jonquils and daffodils rested. I had to ask the question: Who? Who was buried there? Once a detective, always a detective.

Beneath the grey stone lay Katherine Dryden, beloved wife of Harry Dryden, twin sister of the late Arthur Beasley.

She too had died recently within a few weeks of her brother. I went back to Mrs Armitage's memorial: she too had died not long after in that dangerous period last year. If the man with the flowers was Harry Dryden then I began to see what he meant.

I walked back towards the church, meaning to look around it, but when I tried the door it was locked. The glass in the windows looked old, with soft delicate colours. I must ask Mary about the church, she was good about dates and origins.

A soft sleet was beginning to fall as I turned towards the pub and to lunch with Bill Damiani. I had always meant to go back.

*

10

The barman greeted me as I arrived at the Red Dragon. 'Let me take you wet coat, madam.' Clearly the magic cast upon me by Mary was still hanging over me. 'They've gone through,' he said. 'Waiting at the table for you. Mr Damiani has just arrived.'

I thought he might have done: a dark blue Bentley was parked outside. Nothing can make a Bentley look flashy but Billy Damiani had done his best by having the car registration number BBD 1 (he must have paid a lot for that number) and leaving a crocodile briefcase on the front seat with his initials on it in gold. Next to it was a cashmere overcoat, initials here too on the silk lining. He deserved to have it stolen. I made up my mind that Billy Damiani certainly needed looking into. Anyone who scattered their initials around so prodigally must have something to hide. It was interesting too that he had taken the trouble to be more than punctual, he arrived early.

The dining room was small and fairly crowded. The scent of money floated upwards mingling with the freesias from the bowls on the tables.

I walked in with something of defiance, aware that although my jeans and tweed jacket were perfectly in order, the mud on my shoes was not, and my hair was the wrong length.

The woman at the table nearest the door was wearing jeans too but she had a pair of Gucci shoes on with them (well-polished chestnut) and a matching sack bag slung over her shoulder. She looked impossibly chic.

Mary and Damiani were seated at a table in the window overlooking the river. Bill stood up when he saw me.

'Such politeness,' I said under my breath.

He took my hand. 'Charmian, lovely to see you again.' Billy Damiani was tall, with slightly curly dark brown hair, and bright blue eyes. He had a gentle, beautiful voice which he knew how to use, and he was loaded with charm up to his eyeballs. I didn't trust him an inch.

But it was uncouth to appear sour, so I smiled back

11

and sat down. I thought Lady Mary seemed relieved. Walked off your paddy, then? her look said. I gave her a look in return which said: Not as much as you think.

'The church seems interesting,' I said as I unfolded my napkin of stiff linen and a fair indicator of the size of the bill to come. 'But it was locked so I couldn't get in.' I watched as Billy filled my glass with the pale wine they were already drinking.

'Yes, it would be,' said Mary. 'They've had a bit of trouble in the village lately with robberies.' She let Billy refill her glass. Which of us was going to be driving home, I thought, watching Mary. We had come in her car. It had better be me. I noticed Billy was drinking abstemiously. That was certainly his style too; let the others do the drinking, he would do the watching.

'The church looks old.'

'Not as old as the village, that's been here for ever, but the first church was Saxon and there's a bit of it left in the crypt, the present building is Norman.' Mary had taken in architectural styles and a certain amount of history with her mother's milk.

'Who was St Edwin the Martyr?'

Mary looked vague. 'I think he was a Saxon king and someone in his court did him in.'

'And I found Mrs Armitage's grave. She must have had quite a history.'

'The Duke was very genuine, no money but a real title, the earldom was a bit suspect, and gave the family pause for thought. Not quite out of *Debrett*,' said Mary with the detachment of one whose family title is authentic if not very ancient or distinguished, 'but you can call yourself anything, I suppose. He claimed it was an old Scots earldom, Bea knew the score, of course, but she didn't mind. I believe he was madly attractive, not that I ever knew him, he was dead before I was born, and Bea couldn't resist.'

Like aunt, like niece, I thought.

12

'Lot of deaths about the same time as your aunt's,' I said.

'Oh, well, you know what villages are like,' said Mary vaguely.

I didn't, but I supposed I would learn.

'Things go about,' she said, as if death was like gossip and could be transmitted with the post and the groceries. Perhaps it could.

'Was it an epidemic of some sort?'

Mary didn't seem to want to talk about it. 'No, not in Bea's case, she took ill and died. I suppose it was the same with the others.'

An epidemic of death then?

'A man was laying flowers on the grave of a Mrs Dryden, she was a sister of the other three, Beasley, they were called.'

'Local names,' said Mary. She shifted uneasily in her seat. 'Of course, I don't know the village that well.'

'So you're thinking of moving to Brideswell?' Billy Damiani was giving me the full dose of charm. I was being targeted by a first-class performer who wanted me to know it. Perplexing.

'Yes.' I found I had made up my mind. 'I'll be putting an offer in for the house, Mary.' It would be my bolt-hole, my charming, desirable eighteenth-century retreat. I would be like some character in a Jane Austen novel. It was my fantasy.

Billy was ordering smoked salmon for us. 'I hear you are getting married. My friend Humphrey Kent.'

Humphrey would be interested in that description, I thought. I didn't answer, just smiled. Maybe yes, maybe no, we're still negotiating and nothing to do with you. Billy was making me angry.

But Mary had been right about the food, which was delicious. A kind of chicken roulade succeeded the salmon, and then a sorbet. I ate with appreciation. I had had a difficult year, one in which good food had not

13

played much of a part. I had got used to grabbing a hamburger or a toasted sandwich before rushing on to the next crisis, the next meeting. Crime had been increasing in my region. I had been involved personally in at least two cases, and been approached by a multiple wife-murderer and swindler who had thought I looked a promising prospect but who had underestimated me. He was now in prison. Through all these months I had driven myself hard. The savage death yesterday of a man under arrest had not helped. I was conscious of too many rough edges.

Good food was a great emollient, though. Mary and Billy chattered away about friends they had in common, politely including me when they could. Some of the time, I sat quietly listening, letting my own thoughts roam.

I could see the blood on the face of the man who had died, still see his disintegrating features. I had not killed him but certainly he had died because of what I had discovered about him. Over my thoughts I could hear Billy speaking.

'I need your help, Charmian.' I had never liked my own name and I liked it that bit less for it being on his tongue.

Billy ran his finger around the rim of his coffee cup, and lowered his blue gaze.

I stiffened; I felt myself do it, and Billy looked up and saw. He didn't miss much, I thought, as he looked down again.

'Go on.' There is no such thing as a free lunch.

He still did not meet my eye, but let his gaze roam around the room. 'I was here to dinner last week. Brought a girl.'

Surprise me, I thought. Mary's expression did not change, not for one moment had she thought she represented anything important in Billy's life.

'Started the meal, we had a bit of a discussion, she got up and went off. Of course, I thought she'd come back,

14

so I waited. She didn't come back. Never has. Not that night nor the next day. I haven't seen her since. No one has, she's missing.'

I sat thinking. 'When you say discussion, do you mean quarrel?'

'I didn't quarrel, her voice got a bit loud.' He looked round the room. 'You can ask the waiters, they heard. They saw her go.'

'So what did you do?'

'As I said I waited, then went out to ask, the doorman said she had taken her wrap, a scrap of chiffon, and gone through into the street and started walking. So I looked for her in the village as much as I could. It was dark and wet. In the end I gave it up, left a message with the porter, and drove back to London.'

'Leaving her there?'

He shrugged.

'And next day what did you do?'

'I rang her flat, no luck. Then I tried to find out if she'd gone into work but her colleagues hadn't seen her. She has never been back.'

'What about her family?'

'I don't know them.'

'Oh, that's it then, she's gone to them.'

'Perhaps. But I don't think so.'

'So?'

'One of the girls in her flat went to the police. They said she was an adult, not a child, and would probably turn up.'

'Is that all?'

'No. A detective constable came to question me. I don't think he took it seriously.'

I thought that the London police had taken it quite seriously if a detective had called and Billy Damiani knew it. It was this that was what was worrying him. He confirmed this with his next remark.

'Apparently her bank card and chequebook are still in

the flat. He told me that. This was something they did not like.'

I wondered what he most worried about: the fate of his girlfriend, or what would be turned up in his own life if an investigation was launched.

'I don't know what I can do, it's out of my area.'

'The village is in it.' Just, I thought, and how well informed you are.

'What's the girl's name?'

'Chloe Devon.'

I finished my wine. 'Right. If the name comes up, if I hear anything, then I'll let you know.'

Billy was brave enough to articulate one of his worries. 'If anything has happened to Chloe, if she's dead, where would I be?'

'In trouble,' I said readily.

I drove Mary back to Windsor. I was safer at the wheel. By this time the big blue Bentley was speeding its way to London to where Billy Damiani had his home and his office. I would be interested to know what went on in that office. I could consult some of my City friends.

'You can move in when you like,' Mary said as she settled herself in to her seat next to me. 'I'm Bea's executor. I would be her heir if she'd had anything to leave but debts. I'll fix it with the solicitors. You can have a nominal lease before buying.'

'Thanks.'

'Humphrey won't like it, but that's up to you.'

'He won't mind.' I knew he would, but he must learn to bear things like that if he wanted me.

'You're quite ruthless.' Mary closed her eyes comfortably.

'So are you. You fed me, alive, to Billy Damiani.'

She didn't answer.

'And I may not be much use to him.'

What had happened to Chloe Devon? Had she been

16

abducted? Was she dead? Or had the girl just taken off for purposes of her own?

She might be dead, but if her body did not turn up in my patch – and praise be it would not – then I would know as much or as little about her death as colleagues in another Force might transmit. They were supposed to inform me, but knew how to be economical with the truth, having invented the process long before any high-ranking civil servant.

And what did Billy Damiani know about Chloe's disappearance? Rather more than he was telling me, I was sure.

Mary and I had established a wary relationship after the initial trauma of her efforts to get me into professional trouble. We were friends, but careful friends. She was a lot younger than me, so I found myself able to forgive her a good deal. Some residual maternal instinct, I suppose. She had been jealous of my relationship with Humphrey Kent, and probably was still if she admitted it.

'Your trouble,' I said, 'is that you are always dreaming of a Fairy Prince.'

'I'd settle for a real one. Or a royal duke, but they are in short supply.'

She had not heard what Damiani had said to me as he held my car door; he was shivering slightly in the cold wind, the cashmere overcoat still locked in his Bentley. 'I'd take it friendly if you'd help me.' And when I did not answer, he added: 'After all, we all need friends. You might yourself.'

It was nicely said, as mild and sweet as good butter, but I knew a threat when I heard one. A threat mingled with a warning.

As I drove, I asked myself what help, what warning, was he offering?

I ran over what was happening in my life. I had come close to alarms in the past in my work, most police officers

17

do if they aren't pasteboard figures, but there was nothing at the moment. Professionally and privately my conscience was clear, there was no bubble floating over my head saying *Watch it.*

Several days passed, but the name of Chloe Devon did not figure in any reports. Billy Damiani telephoned once to say he had heard nothing from her, and again to say he thought the Met were now taking it seriously. I learnt that this was so, but they had nothing.

I paid a deposit on the house in Brideswell and arranged for a survey to be done; I knew the result would be bad, the roof was certainly in trouble, but I needed to know the worst.

I saw Humphrey several times and told him about the house, and as predicted he was not pleased, but he didn't say much. He was a man of property himself and approved of property owners but I suppose, at heart, he wanted to be the one who chose my property.

He pointed out that he had a house in Windsor and a place in the country so why, when married, did we need another?

Very reasonable and hard to answer. I agreed that I might give up my house in Maid of Honour Row, but I wasn't sure if I wanted to live in his house. I'd think about it. Meanwhile, I took him to Brideswell to see the house and he admitted it had charm. We left the car by the Red Dragon and walked through the village together.

I had visited often enough by now to name a few of my neighbours. Next door, in one of the larger grander houses, lived Crick Leicester and David Cremorne. David was the young cousin of the Earl, still living but in a warmer clime. The estate was kept up but he never came to it. David lived in a Grace and Favour house belonging to the estate. For which, as he told me himself, he paid no rent, but coped with all the maintenance. It was a lovely house, he said, but they did have a problem with rats. He had just written a prize-winning biography of Stanley Baldwin, and was now about to embark on Lord Curzon. He had had a lot of publicity on the television and was modestly famous.

Crick was his stepfather. The two men were both tall and moved beautifully; the stepfather had influenced the style of the son. But Crick was thin, with a wispy grey moustache, and almost bald, with just a few strands of blackish hair, while David was handsome with the famous fire-red Cremorne hair.

David's mother had been the daughter of 'the old Lord', but owing to the law of primogeniture had inherited little money and had been a spender rather than a maker. She had died in Italy where they had lived near Lucca. The estate had been inherited by the son of the younger brother of the 'old Lord' who never came to England and whom no one knew.

Mary had told me about them. 'Aunt Bea liked them but she seemed to think they were a bit of a joke, she always smiled when she spoke of them.' Mary had added reflectively: 'Of course, that may have been due to David's lovely blue eyes and curly hair, Aunt Bea did like a good-looking man. She knew most of the Cremone men in the old days, and I have thought she might have had a bit of a fling with the old Earl.' An amused look had appeared on Mary's own face then. 'And I have a sneaking idea that she knew Crick in his bohemian days . . . he's an artist who doesn't paint.' A definite grin appeared on her face, and I was predisposed to like the two men.

Further down the road lived Nora Garden, an elderly actress. She lived alone, more or less, give or take the odd lover, for she had by no means given up the pleasures of life. A few doors along lived a husband and wife who had not lived here long and who, in the village phrase, 'kept themselves to themselves', and were accordingly, regarded as mysteries. He was a lawyer and she was a

19

civil servant, thus much the village had discovered about Brenda and William Letts. Down one attractive alley was a charming thatched cottage where, so I was told, Dr Harlow lived. He had no surgery in the village, but was a member of a group practice with a health centre on the outskirts of Reading. If you were very sick, the doctor came out to you, otherwise you took yourself and your ailments in on the bus or got a friend to drive you in. I saw Dr Harlow one day, a tall, quiet-looking man who was walking his Jack Russell terriers with the patient air that owners of dogs soon learn. After that, I saw him several times with his dogs, walking under the trees beyond the church.

The vet, a handsome young man called Tim Abbey and known locally as 'our Tim', came regularly in his white van because this was a farming village. In addition the same white van set up its hospital once a week near the church for small pets. It was well patronized. In fact it was easier to be a sick animal than a sick person.

But there was competition. I knew from my Windsor friends Birdie Peacock and Winifred Eagle, retired witches now into faith healing and homoeopathy, that one of their band of white witches lived in Brideswell. She and her husband lived in the Midden, Ruddles Lane, and cured all, four-footed, winged, and otherwise, who needed help. I had not yet located the Midden, but had to assume that, sited as it was near the old village rubbish tip, it was tucked away somewhere out of sight since even a medieval village would put it at a distance. Birdie had pursed her lips at the mention of Ellen and Jack Bean. He was no good, she hinted, and the marriage of Ellen had put her out of the witch business. White witches were better unmarried, and most certainly better without spouses like Jack the rogue, she implied.

'It's a sink for money, that house.' Humphrey said, 'you'll spend a fortune doing it up.'

'I'll do it gradually.'

20

'I can see you're determined.'

'Yes, I am.'

'I suppose I'll see you through this stage too,' he said, half in joke, half grimly.

'Don't look down on me.' That was a joke too, because I am not that much shorter than he is. I'm tall for a woman, which has helped me in my profession. I'm a former gingerhead whose colour has toned down nicely with years. He is a bit grey. I have lost (or think I have) my Scottish accent, Humphrey speaks the Queen's English with the slightly husky voice of an ex-smoker.

I had known Humphrey for about five years and although it had been pretty obvious within a few minutes of our meeting what we felt about each other and what we would do about it, it had taken longer to add friendship to the equation.

My fault, I think. I was prickly and on my guard. I had had an early marriage with friendship and respect and not much of any passion, and a subsequent relationship that was full of emotions but with certainly no respect of either side, and I didn't believe either mix a good base for a marriage. I wanted something better. Humphrey had been married once before and all I knew about that was that she was Lotty and had wanted a more socially active life. I had been promised a look at Lotty but so far had never seen her.

So I waited. The friendship started to grow stronger when I was threatened with an illness. Although neither of us talked about it much, I knew I had all the strength and love there that I needed. And when a searing, tearing case ended with me close to becoming the butt of chauvinistic police humour, he had seen me through that maze and shown me how to fight back. So the friendship was there all right.

But in my mind the relationship was like a reel of cotton that was always unwinding and that I couldn't get to the end of: I was half curious, half afraid. I didn't

21

think we'd kill each other, but you never can tell. So there it was, this marvellous relationship with everything, present and potential, and I was still holding back.

Brideswell was quiet the day I took Humphrey to walk down the village street. I noticed the baker's shop was called Dryden, and that a Beasley ran the Post Office, but somehow I could not associate the man I had met in the churchyard as either a baker or a postmaster.

Chloe Devon might have walked down this street and then vanished.

'I'm off to Brussels next week,' Humphrey said as we drove back to Windsor. His own life was full of mysterious journeys about which one was not meant to enquire too much, while on the other hand I often felt he was shockingly well informed about what went on in my professional life. That was something I didn't like too much.

'That's it, I suppose,' I said. 'Why I want this house . . . when you are away I want to miss you in a house of my own and not yours.'

Thirteen days after my luncheon with Billy and Mary, I saw in a fax from one of the Met areas with which my communication was good and working well that a bundle of women's clothes had been found in west London. A short black dress of very good quality – the label was torn out but it had been new and expensive – and the underclothes to go with it. No shoes, no tights, no handbag. The speculation was that the clothes belonged to Chloe Devon.

I did not, at the time, tell either Mary or Billy Damiani.

I spent the late afternoon at a committee in London, and got back to find a message from Humphrey on my answer-machine.

'About Brideswell . . . Don't move there. Cut your losses and run.'

Run? What was I supposed to be running from?

And then I checked myself, and thought again. I played

the message back. It wasn't Humphrey's voice, it was not all that much like his. What was the matter with me, that I should immediately decide it was?

But if it wasn't him, who was it? And was that person pretending to be Humphrey?

A joke . . . ? Some of my colleagues had that sort of sense of humour, I regret to say. Or a real warning?

TWO

I took advantage of a quiet afternoon on the next day to drive myself round the wooded and hilly countryside in which Brideswell lay. From one high point I could look down on the village.

I could see the shape of the village street, observe the church tower, the doctor's house seen distantly over the trees, and right on the edge of the area, down wooded lanes, the animal clinic. To the west lay the hospital, and beyond that, the microbiological research station.

There was a ghost already abroad in Brideswell although I did not know it.

Not a walking, talking, seen on the streets sort of ghost but a haunting none the less.

The whole village knew but were not talking about it. When I say the whole village, I except the parson, who did not know and whom nobody told; the village thought innocence was his job. All the people I was getting to know, like Crick and David, Ellen Bean and Thomas Dryden, all were aware of the ghost, but saw no reason to tell me. Ghosts were not my business.

This was not to say that all who knew about the ghost cared about the ghost. Brideswell was a down to earth working village, and although they might know it was, in a sense, a haunted village, it was something they could shrug off. You don't have to see the ghost just because you live in a haunted village. Most of them had other and more practical worries. The current recession in farming and in the local industries was more important to these pragmatic people. In fact, if the haunting brought trade to the village they would be pleased.

These villagers knew that ghosts only existed in people's minds, and were fuelled by people's imagination, so that if you kept your own mind closed then you were safe. Such villagers were the baker and his wife, the doctor and the vet. In fact, the vet, who only came in and out, had no notion of the haunting and would not have minded if he had done, being more concerned with the valuable minks and sables he was trying to breed.

It was not an old ghost, it had not been around for very long, a new young phantom in an ancient village which had certainly known other ghosts. Those old ghosts had died away, leaving not even a memory behind. None of those old ghosts, legacies of ancient quarrels, ancient wounds, had done any harm, or if they had then years had buried the memory of it.

It was a he–she ghost, which Ellen Bean was later to tell me was quite usual and rather nasty.

But because it wasn't a walking, talking, visible ghost didn't mean it wasn't an eating ghost. This was a new, hungry ghost.

This was a murderous ghost.

THREE

I visited the house in Brideswell at irregular intervals, gradually moving in a few of my possessions, and camping out there while I decided on a scheme of decoration. My goddaughter Kate, now married to George Rewley, a young detective whom I had just appointed to my own Investigation Unit, fancied her skills in interior decoration and would have been glad to help. But she would have taken over and I wanted this place, wallpaper, paint, curtains, and all, to reflect my own choice.

As I went to the village, buying bread in the baker's and choosing coffee in the general store, I realized that the Met had been in and about the area enquiring about Chloe Devon. They had come into my area unobtrusively, but they had been there. No co-operation from me or the appropriate Windsor police unit had been requested. That interested me, but I did not complain, although I would do so with force when and if it suited me.

By this time I had discovered more about Chloe Devon, and in doing so, had come to learn more about Billy Damiani. To begin with, he was her employer, a fact he had not brought out when we talked. He must have known I would find out.

One of his enterprises (and I was sure he had many more) was a fine art magazine, *Arian*, which was run from an office off Duke Street in Piccadilly. Chloe had worked as a research assistant. Damiani had bought the magazine from its founder who remained as editor. It was said to lose money but had a good reputation in the art world. The prestige factor probably operated for Billy, who got invited into worlds he might not otherwise have penetrated. Windsor Castle, for one.

Chloe was twenty-three (Damiani was forty-three – he didn't look it, must dye his hair) and had taken a degree in French and Art History at Bristol University. Then she had travelled for six months in Italy and France which she had financed by working as a waitress and a courier or whatever came up. She was not a clever girl, the degree was a very average second, but she was pretty, hard working, and good mannered. She was liked by the other research assistants. Billy Damiani eyed all the pretty girls who worked for him, and took them all out in turn – in the media they were called his 'harem' – but Chloe was the first one who had mattered with him.

Both Chloe's parents were several times divorced and remarried with new families and not much interest was taken in Chloe. This had made her, as a friend reported, a 'tough girl'.

She was also, the same friend said, one to take risks, a 'chancer'. There was a hint from this last girl, one Rowena Adams, that Chloe was out for what she could get. Not exactly mercenary, but with a kind of mental price list in her head.

To me, she sounded a mixture of toughness and vulnerability, the very profile of a girl who might walk out into the night and be murdered.

About Billy Damiani, however, I had not discovered very much more than that he was rich, sociable, and ambitious. In what direction his ambitions went opinions varied, just as the stories of his origins did. The received impression was that he had neither been born nor educated in England, while giving a very good imitation of having done so. But he had a lot of solid investments in this country, owned much property, and might be exactly what he appeared to be: a rich social climber who liked living in England. 'If he could marry a duchess or the odd sprig of the royal family, it wouldn't come amiss,' said my informant, an officer in the Met who claimed to know no more than he had told me but who might, just possibly, know the odd fact or two more.

'Don't think he'd blunder into murder, though,' my informant said.

But men like that do, I thought, just as girls like Chloe become their victims.

Damiani telephoned me himself that evening. I wasn't pleased to hear his voice and did not know how he had tracked me down. Mary, I supposed.

He caught me at the house in Brideswell where I was talking to Crick and David whom I was beginning to know and like. They had been giving me a hand with moving some bits of furniture into the sitting room. A long bookcase had given us trouble and we were pausing for breath.

I had put a match to the fire and the leaping flames were casting shadows on the wall that I had painted white.

The bookcase was stranded in the middle of the room. There was a space in the wall opposite the window all ready for it, but we didn't seem able to get it into position.

David was awarding it an assessing survey. 'If we give a shove to the left, I think we shall have it.'

They were the only inhabitants of the village who had come forward in a friendly way. The rest were, understandably, keeping their distance. My reputation had gone before me: I was a police officer, a certain notoriety hung around me, danger could follow. They were wary, nervous, watching me while they saw how things worked out. And the disappearance of Chloe Devon played its part in this carefulness.

When the telephone rang, the instrument was stranded on the other side of the bookcase, and I had to crawl round to answer it.

Billy Damiani sounded tense. 'Oh, good, you are there.

28

You were such a long time answering that I thought you couldn't be.'

'There was a reason for that.' I sat back on my heels, hoping he would not talk too long, it was cold and draughty on the floor.

'I wondered if you had any news for me. Of Chloe, I mean. I know some of her clothes were found. I identified them. I wish it hadn't been me. I felt strong suspicious breaths down my neck. He had a very mean look, that detective.'

'Don't let it worry you.' I could see that Crick and David were listening to every word, while pretending to adjust the angle of the bookcase. If they weren't careful it would tilt on to me. 'Watch it, David,' I said.

'Have you got someone with you?' asked Damiani nervously.

'Only furniture movers,' I said. 'Don't let it worry you, carry on.'

'I've been hoping she would turn up . . . but finding her clothes . . . that was nasty.'

'It doesn't look good.'

'You can say that again . . . I wish she'd walk into the room, alive and well. I'd give anything not to have taken her out that night, and not to have had an argument with her.'

'What did you quarrel about?'

Hastily he set me right. 'Not a quarrel, just different points of view.'

'What about?'

'Nothing really, this and that, you know how it is sometimes.'

'She got up and walked out,' I pointed out. 'She felt strongly enough to do that.'

'Too strongly, it was stupid,' he said reluctantly. 'She was jealous, a bit possessive, poor girl. Nothing in it. Not for me, not for her.'

'Was she blackmailing you?' I asked bluntly. Over the

top of the bookcase I saw a look of passionate interest cross Crick's face, only to be quickly repressed.

'No, of course not, nothing to blackmail me on . . . If you must know, she wanted promotion at work and I couldn't promise that . . . And she got annoyed, thought I could have done it for her, but I don't interfere in that kind of way. If she was good, she would get there anyway, I told her.'

'And then she walked out?'

'Right.'

And I didn't blame her, I thought, it was damn patronizing. But where did she go?

'She had a lot of friends,' he was saying. 'She got about. She must have met someone she knew and gone off with them. Probably in Bermuda by now.'

Without her clothes?

Billy said, 'Let me know, won't you, if any news comes in? I just have this feeling she *will* turn up.'

I went back to the fire. 'Let's have a drink. Dry sherry or whisky?'

'Whisky for me, please.' David looked at his stepfather, and Crick nodded, before putting another log on the fire. I had discovered for myself what he already knew, that log fires need constant attention and can be hard work. 'And for him too.'

I poured myself some dry sherry. 'Why did no one see the girl walking through the village?' It was as if she had taken off on a flying carpet.

Neither of them made any effort to hide that they knew what I had been talking about on the telephone.

'It was a cold, wet night,' said Crick. 'And a big football match on the TV. Most people were home watching. The village is quiet at night.' And dark. There were no street lights, only the lamps behind curtained windows.

'She was wearing a short black dress and very high heels, no coat, just a little flyaway wrap. She must have been an unusual sight in the village street.'

30

'Someone may have seen her and be keeping quiet. People don't always tell the truth.'

'Or she may have gone up one of the side-streets. Or a car may have picked her up,' said David.

'Perhaps.' Billy had said the same thing. He put it badly but in a way he got it right.

I had a camp bed which I set up in front of the fire and I spent the night with the fire crackling and the flames making patterns on the wall. I thought about the girl walking out into the night and disappearing like a little lost cat. It made me shiver.

When I got back to Windsor, I found a report that a woman's arm, a young woman's arm, had been discovered in rough ground near Waterloo. It had been wrapped in a black plastic bag of the sort that gardeners use and hidden under a pile of leaves where a dog had found it. But the rats had found it first.

It was not immediately identifiable as Chloe's arm, and in fact since the fingertips had been chewed away, it was not going to be easy to identify it at all, but it appeared to be the arm of a young and slender woman so the chances were that it was Chloe's.

Nothing to do with me, I thought, found on the Met's territory, it was their body. I would hear about it, but I need take no action, I wasn't on Damiani's payroll.

I waited but nothing more turned up.

Two days later, the south of England was ravaged by strong winds. Windsor got the full force. The cat and I sat together on the stairs in the house in Maid of Honour Row and listened to the gale raging in from the sea. The houses shook with the force, the windows rattled. Suddenly there was a roar, the back door blew open and the wind was inside with us.

It tore round the house and up the stairs, pushing me aside and banging into furniture. Then it loosened its grip

31

and I battled out to close and lock the back door, still miraculously on its hinges.

For a moment there was silence, then the winds screamed on us again, louder and stronger than ever. I heard a cracking noise above me and the sound of falling glass. I crawled up the stairs and saw that my bedroom window had been fractured, there was glass all over the carpet.

That was the climax of the storm. Slowly the wind relaxed and silence and quiet came back. Muff and I went to bed, ignoring the open window. There seemed to be plaster and debris on the bed, but I was too tired to care.

Next morning it was clear that Windsor had caught it badly, and Maid of Honour Row looked as if a bomb had dropped on it. My windows were out and my roof was damaged. When I looked up through my cracked bedroom ceiling, I could see the sky.

I was insured but it would take time. The builder called to assess the damage and was not optimistic. 'Going to take a while,' he said. 'Half Windsor is calling on me to put the roof back on.'

He was a small wiry man wearing dark spectacles and carrying a notebook in which he made little scribbles and diagrams as he went around the house.

'Not the Queen, I suppose?'

'No, not her,' he replied seriously. 'She's all right up there on the hill, built strong the castle is. Besides, she's got other places to go, hasn't she? No, you'll have to take your turn. I can rig a tarpaulin up to keep the water out.' It had already started to rain. 'But you'll have to wait. I've got mothers and babies and little old ladies on my list and they must come first.'

I thought about offering a bribe but decided that was not my style, and it may not have been what he was hoping for.

As he left, he said: 'You've got a bit of subsidence too, by the look of it. Better get that done at the same time.'

32

I could see that once in, he was going to be with me for weeks. Possibly months. He had come highly recommended as an honest man, but I decided I would get both an estimate of the cost and a survey. We were clearly in for a long relationship and it had better be a good one.

He confirmed this thought with his next words: 'Take my advice, go and stay with a friend and let me get on with it nice and easy, and I won't worry you.'

I walked round the corner to see my friends, the neighbourhood witches, Winifred and Birdie, to find out how they had fared, and discovered without surprise they had escaped all damage.

Entirely due, said Birdie, to having foreseen the storm coming and having had the right protective spells to cast around their house.

'I wish you had done the same for me, then.'

Birdie shook her head. 'You must have faith, and that's not in you, dear.'

It was true that my life and career had not encouraged in me faith in much except dogged hard work.

'So what will you do, Charmian?' asked her companion witch, Winifred Eagle. 'Come to us if you like, we'd love to have you.'

'No. Thanks, but I shall go out to the house in Brideswell.' True, the unknown telephone caller had advised against it, but I had made up my mind without conscious thought.

'Oh, you can't live there by yourself, dear.' This was Birdie. 'Would you like to take the dog?' We shared ownership of the dog, but he preferred them to me. She looked down at the dog, comfortably asleep by the fire, the storm had not stressed him either. 'You'd like that, Ben, wouldn't you?' Ben wagged his tail without opening his eyes.

'I won't be on my own, or not all the time.' I had the intention of sending Humphrey a message: if you want to see me, come out to Brideswell. If you want to stay in the country, stay there with me. In my house. You might call it an ultimatum. 'I shall take the cat.'

I didn't know what Humphrey would answer, but it would be unexpected, he usually managed to surprise me. Then I left a message for my assistant saying that I would be staying in the country, that I would be absent from my office today, but he could always get me on the telephone, he had my number.

I piled all the possessions I wanted with me, the books I was reading, the notes I was making for a book I was writing, country clothes, and some food, into my car; I put Muff in her basket and set out for Brideswell.

I was going to take possession of my property.

I was well on the road to Brideswell, with Muff keening by my side, before the thought came to me that the village too had been in the path of the storm with consequent damage to the houses there. I might be going to ruin worse than I had left behind.

Trees were down on either side of the lane which led to the village with branches thrown across the road, mute testimony to a wild night. But now the sky was blue and tranquil, the air calm.

I passed down the village street, seeing with relief that it looked unscathed. None of the houses had lost even a window whereas Windsor had looked bombed. There was the church, and the Red Dragon, all as normal, and there was my house.

A small bush had come from nowhere to rest on my garden wall, a laburnum tree that stood near the house was tilted at an angle, and a broken flowerpot lay on the patch of grass, but the house stood as it always had.

I unlocked the door, hurried to push the button that started the heating. I hauled in my cases and then gave Muff her freedom, offering her words of advice about watching the traffic and remembering the way back. But she showed no sign of wanting to rush outside. On the

34

contrary, she leapt up to the top of the bookcase and looked at me with a sad and sombre face.

Snug within its thick stone walls, the house soon warmed up. I lit the fire in the hearth downstairs, the bottle of sherry still stood on the bookcase with a glass ready and waiting. I poured myself a drink, then stood by the fire enjoying the heat.

It was very quiet; I realized how little I had of silence in my life and how easy it was to enjoy it. Never before, in my working life, had I deliberately taken time off. But I was doing it now. I admitted to myself that I had wanted to come here to this house and that the storm had given me the chance.

Standing by the fire, I could see through the window to the street, catch a sight of the church and a good view of the Red Dragon. Only a few cars parked outside. Trade must be poor today.

The telephone did not ring, no one called, I did not exist. I felt weightless.

I ate my lunch sitting by the fire, reading. Muff stayed where she was. We ignored each other but I could tell by the occasional sharp twitch of her tail that she was not pleased with her move.

Then suddenly, she leapt down and disappeared through a half-open door. I ignored that too, I knew that all outer doors and window were closed and she could not get lost.

Lured out by the sun, I walked through the village towards the church. A few people had now emerged with shopping baskets and dogs to walk; I could see customers in the shops. Life was picking up after the storm. I saw some faces I felt I would like to get to know, but no one spoke to me. I was studied though, an object of interest as the new owner of Mrs Armitage's house.

On my right was the house where Crick Leicester and David Cremorne lived. I thought about ringing their door bell but decided against it. Today I wanted to be solitary.

35

I walked up to the church, undamaged by the winds. It was open now, and I entered to meet the usual smell of furniture polish and brass polish and flowers. Damp as well, and very cold.

The wall were lined with memorial plaques, most in honour of the Barons Cremorne. I walked slowly past, reading them where they were in English as my Latin was not up to translating the earlier inscriptions. They seemed to have got their start in the mid-eighteenth century, so there must have been an earlier owner of the manor and estate before them. Or they had married the heiress, and the estate had passed with the female line.

A prolific lot, I thought as I read, with sons and daughters in comfortable numbers.

Quite a few Drydens about too, I saw, and some buried in great style with splendid stone statuary. They were probably an older family than the Cremornes, and perhaps once had been considerable landowners, possibly even owning the manor itself. An estate as old as this one must have passed through the hands of many families.

I amused myself with the romantic Thomas Hardyish notion of a noble family now reduced to poverty.

Of course, the man I had seen on that other visit had not looked poor, nor spoken like a farm worker; he had been classless, hard to pin down.

I looked down the length of the church towards the altar. The figure that I had seen in the distance was moving down the aisle towards me, where it turned into Ellen Bean, white witch.

She was carrying a duster and a tin of brass polish. She seemed as surprised to see me as I was to see her.

'Hello, Mrs Bean. I didn't expect to see you here.'

'My week for cleaning the altar brass.'

That was something I hadn't expected either. How did white witches feel about altars and crosses?

She picked up my thought. 'It's a very old church, Norman, Saxon, and before that there would have been

36

a temple here. It's very old and very sacred, this ground. You can feel it. Or if you're sensitive, then you can. I feel it very strongly. Do you?' I shook my head wordlessly. 'Oh, well, not everyone can. Birdie said not to expect too much.' Thank you, Birdie, I thought. Then she patted one of the pews as if it should have its share of her benediction. 'Besides, whatever deity comes here, He' – she paused, then added thoughtfully – 'or She, will want it nice and shining. And that's my job.'

A kind of housemaid to the gods, I thought.

'And my Jack's a churchwarden.'

'So he is.' I remembered seeing his name. Jack Bean and Ermine Sprott.

'But I like doing it, I enjoy a nice bit of bright brass. It pays for the rubbing. Miss Garden does the flowers when she's here, she's more artistic than I am. But she's away at the moment on tour so the vicar does them himself, and a poor hand at arranging them he is.'

'Some old families here,' I said, as we paced down the aisle towards the door, passing a Dryden memorial tablet. 'Lot of Drydens and Beasleys.'

'It's a funny village,' she said obliquely. 'Bean and I aren't local. Bean's a Reading man but he's quite a countryman at heart, goes rabbiting and has a dear little ferret; and I come from Oxford. I said a special prayer when we moved into the Midden.'

'Did you think that necessary?'

'Not necessary, just a precaution. But don't you worry. You'll be all right where you are, that house can look after itself.'

After this somewhat unnerving remark she gave me a kind of bob as if I was the Queen and sped off down a side aisle to the vestry.

I walked home, stopping only at the Post Office to get some stamps and then on to the baker's to choose a loaf. I thought I'd seen the last of Ellen Bean for the day, but she was there outside the baker's shop.

In my experience, witches tend to be tall and thin with an air of fly-away thinness, at least Winifred and Birdie were like that, but Ellen was short and muscular. But she possessed the same sharp observing eye that my two Windsor friends had, like a bird fixing on a likely worm, and I recognized the expression now. She bent her head to pick up the worm.

'You're looking for that girl?'

'It's not my case. Really nothing to do with me.' Not exactly true, since Billy Damiani had tried to engage my interest. The village knew I was a high-ranking police officer but had no idea of how I worked and what my powers were. Damiani got closer to it, he knew I had power, but even he did not really know.

Because all information about major crimes came into my unit, my important-sounding title might have meant that I was no more than a super collater. Possibly this is what the powers that be had had in mind when they offered me the post. Perhaps they had it in mind to sideline an irritating and ambitious woman, but they had reckoned without me. I had now established my own small investigating unit: I could initiate an enquiry.

Billy Damiani knew this much, and was trying to use me. But I was using him: to establish the extension of my powers I needed a successful case. The missing Chloe even might provide it.

Ellen heard what I said but did not accept it. 'Oh.' A look of surprise crossed her face. 'Being a woman, I thought it would be you.'

'I don't specialize in cases involving women.'

'This will be . . .' She spoke as if she was sure. 'You won't find her.'

'I think she'll turn up,' I said cautiously. The loaf was still warm, they must bake on the premises, unusual these days. It smelt delicious, yeasty and wholesome. I was suddenly hungry. I felt like tearing off a corner and chewing it.

'Not in one piece.' Ellen Bean spoke with conviction. I didn't answer, because I agreed with her.

All the same, she should not know about the finding of the clothes and the arm because the information had not been released. I had observed before from Birdie and Winifred that these white witches were always well informed – and it wasn't telepathy in my opinion. Nor anything paranormal. I thought they ran a very good intelligence network. It might be worth tapping into Mrs Bean's.

She took in my silence. 'You're not going to talk about it, I can see that. Birdie said you wouldn't. Well, you know where to come if you want help. The village doesn't like it, the girl disappeared from this very street you are standing on.'

Prompted by her words, I looked up and down. The street was empty.

'Pity no one saw her go,' I said.

'Not many people out that night, big football match. The doctor or the vet might be on the road. You'll see the vet as you've got a cat.'

So she knew that too? Birdie and Winifred had been busy. She's a very healthy cat,' I said.

Ellen opened the shop door. 'Accidents do happen. Must get my loaf.'

'Wait a minute,' I said. 'As you know the village so well, tell me what the three Beasleys died of.'

She paused, one hand on the door, obviously considering what to say. 'Yes, very nasty, and they kept it very quiet,' she said. 'One of those infections, virus, went through them all and the doctors couldn't help. Some people say it was poison,' she said, her eyes bright. 'But as I say it was kept quiet.'

'But no one else caught it or died of it?'

She considered that too, and decided what to say. 'No, and very glad we were too, it could have gone through the village, decimating us. But they'd been in a bad car accident before and the shock lowered them. An "opportunistic infection", the doctors called it. If it was an infection. They were specially nursed, barrier nursing, and all that, but it didn't do any good. I could have told them it wouldn't, got their name on it, that virus had.' She pushed open the door of the shop.

But I didn't let her get away. 'And then Mrs Dryden died, she was twin sister to Mr Beasley. Did she die of the same thing?'

'No, officially it was a road accident.' She shrugged. 'Supposing it was one of those purposeful accidents?'

'Any reason for her to do that?'

'Missed her brother, I suppose. Twins . . . it's different for them, isn't it?'

Her eyelids veiled her eyes as a bird's do. Something she knew, and something she wouldn't say. Well, it wasn't my business. Nothing in the village except the house was my business. It was not my case.

I went back to my second home and put some more logs on the dying fire. No sign of Muff, usually a keen fire watcher.

'Muff, Muff, where are you?'

She didn't come at my voice as she usually did. I went round the house, calling her name. Upstairs in the bedroom I still had very little furniture, nothing she could hide in. There was my suitcase with a few clothes in it but I hadn't even opened it. The camp bed was standing near the window. I could see a few cat hairs, so she had been there.

I stood by the window, taking in what I had. I would make this room beautiful, it was a room built for elegance. Nothing forced, elaborate or shiny, I decided, but simple country stuff. Antique, if I could afford it. My friend Annie Cooper would help me here. Annie had a very good eye for furniture and although rich herself never encouraged antique dealers to get above themselves. She could bargain with the best.

40

Shivering a little, I went back to the living-room fire. But I had to find Muff, there was no peace for me while she might be lost. I returned to the kitchen.

And there I saw a cupboard door was ajar. I opened it wide to reveal a broom cupboard, now empty except for the smell of polish and damp. Yes, I had to admit there was a smell of damp.

Or was it mice?

It was a deep cupboard built into the wall, sloping slightly downwards. No sign of Muff though. But there was just a stirring of the air that suggested quiet movement.

I looked up, and there, on a high shelf, she was, bright eyed, tail lashing, with a mouse in her mouth. I couldn't speak, ma'am, her eyes said, I've got my mouth full.

The mouse, fortunately, was dead.

Muff slid from the shelf, all limber liquid movement, and disappeared. I let her go. Cat owners know all about nature being red in tooth and claw. Muff, the placid, loving, gentle creature was only domestic as long as it suited her.

I closed the cupboard door, and decided to make some tea.

On the wall by the stove was a bracket where something long had hung leaving only its ghostly outline on the wall. Now the house was heating up, I could tell that this must have been a cosy corner in winter if you were an old lady who did not use the sitting room overmuch. A lovely if battered old rug still rested by the great old Aga which had mercifully been converted to burning gas when the central heating was put in.

Possibly Mrs Armitage had hung something she valued from the bracket. Or it might have held a pot plant. Although from all I had heard of Beatrice Armitage and seen of her garden, she had not been a pot plant admirer.

I made myself a pot of tea, and took it to drink by the fire which was now crackling with flames. Presently, Muff

41

slid into the room to stretch out in the warmth. Neither of us mentioned the mouse.

I was a hunter myself, professionally, but I felt a lot of sympathy with that mouse just then, surrounded as I was by people I couldn't trust.

I don't like you, Billy Damiani, I thought, you use women, you are trying to use me. I wonder if you killed Chloe? I thought of those elegant, well-manicured hands with the heavy gold ring, squeezing the girl's neck until she stopped breathing.

But no, he was too rich and too sophisticated to do it himself. He would hire a killer.

I drank some tea, and ate buttered bread and honey. This might be my case, the one I was looking for.

Women avenge women. I wished I had known Chloe Devon.

I went to bed early, wrapping myself in blankets on the camp bed which I set up in front of the fire. I must see about ordering a bed; I knew a shop the other side of Oxford which made beautiful beds and which would deliver one speedily. I had saved the owner a lot of money from a con man so I knew he would look after me well.

The fire crackled with a comforting voice, Muff deposited herself upon me, we were both tired and both soon asleep.

In the morning I drove into my office on the edge of Windsor. It seemed natural somehow, I hardly thought of Maid of Honour Row.

When I got there, a fax informed me that another arm had been found in New Cross, south London. This arm had been identified as belonging to the girl. On this arm, the fingers still had their pads; the prints matched those in Chloe's flat.

Additional information came with this fax which referred to the first arm found: the pathologist who had given it a first examination was puzzled by the bite marks on the fingers. These, he thought, had not been made by a dog or by rats. He was working on it.

Before I left a leg had been found in a car park in Paddington.

Bits of Chloe were turning up all over London. But no head and no heart.

It was universally acknowledged that whoever had the heart, had the case.

FOUR

Several days passed, and a quick visit to Maid of Honour Row showed me that although the builder had fulfilled his promise of replacing broken window glass and of protecting my roof with tarpaulin, nothing else had been done. Presumably a long queue of aged widows and mothers with babies still stretched ahead of me. I telephoned to get an answerphone message that he was too busy to answer now but would reply when he could, so the rumour passed on by Birdie and Winifred that he had taken off for a holiday in the sun must be false.

But just in case I left a message of my own to remind him to protect his face when he worked on my roof since my medical friends told me that too much sun was dangerous leading to heat stroke and skin cancer. Then I left my telephone number in Brideswell in case he wanted to reply.

My own answering machine had no word from Humphrey, to my secret pique, nor any letters. And he was good at letters.

Billy Damiani however had left several messages: one in the office, and two at Maid of Honour Row. I had nothing to tell him, except what was in the newspapers.

I think Billy Damiani was frightened: he was being questioned almost daily now by the Met as pieces of body turned up (a leg today), but there was nothing I could do for him. 'Let the machine take over,' was all I said.

Every morning I set my alarm to wake me at six, then

I fed Muff, drank some coffee, and took a bath. I was on the road driving to my office in Windsor before seven. The roads were emptier then so I made good time. I usually cut lunch and worked straight through, leaving early to get back to what I was coming to think of as my 'country house'. It was getting to be an addiction. The bed and chairs I had ordered would be arriving today so I had left the key with David Cremorne.

David said it would be a pleasure, he was fascinated to see what I was doing to the house, he knew I was going to be innovative. So far I had not done much. The most innovative thing had been to ask Jack Bean, Ellen's husband, who was the village handyman, to fit a small cat door for Muff. It was an exit she took full advantage of, and I had seen her in the churchyard, tail busy, eyes alert, on the hunt.

There was a car parked in the road outside my house, with David's bike leaning against the garden wall.

A new car, a big BMW, surely not the means by which the bed had been delivered. I knew the man who made the bed had had much success with fashionable customers with a show of his beds and tables in Liberty's but I didn't think he ran a car such as that one.

I parked my own car behind it and opened my front door. Humphrey was sitting by the fire (lit unasked by someone), he had Muff on his knee, and he was talking to David who lounged on the other side. They both looked comfortably at home.

Humphrey had managed to surprise me as usual.

Both men leapt to their feet when they saw me, Humphrey still holding Muff.

I put down my briefcase and shoulder bag. 'You two know each other?'

'I know his book,' said Humphrey.

'He's made some interesting suggestions,' said David with a pleased face. 'If I have the luck to run to a second edition, then I shall use them.'

'And of course, I know your cousin.'

'Oh, really?' David was cautious. 'I've never met him myself. He never comes home from Africa.'

I demanded to know what was uppermost in my mind. 'Did the bed come?'

'It arrived the same moment that I did,' said Humphrey. 'I helped the man in with it.' Yes, he certainly knew how to surprise me.

David was looking at the fire. 'I was here. We all carried it up the stairs and put it together. Tonight you will sleep in state. You didn't say it was a four-poster.'

'Only a small one.' I was a little ashamed of the extravagance. Charmian Daniels, the girl from Dundee, shouldn't own a four-poster bed. 'It seemed right for the house. Did the hangings come with it?'

'Came and are up. Muff helped there.' He looked affectionately at the little cat, still lolling in Humphrey's arms. 'She likes you.'

'Known her a long time.'

I moved towards the table with bottles and glasses. 'Let's have a drink.' I was trying to feel my way, neither of them seemed disposed to be moved from the fire. I wanted a shower and to change out of my working clothes. I was also hungry. I must have looked it, I suppose; Humphrey did know me very well, even better than he knew Muff.

'I've booked a table at the Dragon,' he said. 'Let's all have dinner there.'

'Not me, although I'd love to.' David sounded regretful. 'Crick's cooking a special pheasant casserole. I mustn't keep it waiting either, he gets very tetchy with his cooking.' He stood up to go.

I saw him to the door, and thanked him for his help. 'Pleasure,' he said. 'Some bed.'

I returned to where Humphrey was poking the fire.

'That's a new car,' I said.

'Brought it back with me. You'll like it. It's easy to

drive. Come back and stay with me.' He looked around him. 'You can't live here just yet, you haven't got enough furniture.'

'I'll manage. I've got several pieces, and the bed, don't forget the bed. I'm getting some more. How's your house in Windsor? Did it suffer in the big wind?'

'Not touched.' He put some more wood on the fire. 'I shall sell it, I think. One can be overhoused. Let's talk about it over dinner.'

'I want to ask you about Billy Damiani,' I said as I went upstairs.

'Oh, he's trouble all right,' I heard him mutter.

The two men had placed the bed well, with its back against the wall where I would be able to look out of the window. It had settled into position as if it had always been there.

The hangings were a William Morris print of birds and flowers, inspired but not copied from an Elizabethan embroidered counterpane.

It was ridiculous to have spent so much money, and I didn't even legally own the house yet.

Humphrey had followed me upstairs. 'Nice curtains,' he said. 'You see you can choose things for yourself without asking Kate or Annie Cooper.'

'This wasn't difficult, all the hangings came with the bed.' I hung up my coat. All I had was a peg on the wall, not even a proper hook. Somewhere to put my clothes must be attended to next. I smoothed the coat lovingly, it was cashmere. I still valued cashmere as if I was still that youngster from Dundee who hadn't got much. 'I was surprised to see you here today. I didn't expect you.'

'You did leave a message saying you were staying here. Besides, I was worried about you.'

'About me?' I was surprised again. It was agreed that I was good at looking after myself. That I expected to and didn't want help was a tacit agreement.

47

'The wind.'

'I wasn't touched. The house yes, but not me. Nor Muff.'

'I felt I could trust Muff to survive,' he said drily.

'You can trust me.' I added, lightly, since I hadn't meant it seriously, 'Even though I have had a telephone call warning me off living in Brideswell. Someone in the village who doesn't like me, I suppose. Not all country people relish townees moving in.' And perhaps even fewer liked police officers. 'But I promise you I can look after myself. Been doing it for years.'

'I wish I believed that. I remember some of the things you've got yourself into.'

'I'm a reformed character.'

'I wish you weren't involved with Damiani.'

'I'm not involved with him.'

'He sticks to things and people.'

Mary had said something like that. 'Not to me,' I answered, really believing it.

He didn't answer. 'I've got something for you.' He produced a red leather box, a box of fine old morocco. 'Open it.'

Inside was a large sapphire surrounded with a ring of diamonds. It was a beautiful ring, a dream of a ring, but it was a young girl's ring, I couldn't wear it.

I wanted it, of course, what woman wouldn't want a ring like that, but it was not for me. I looked down at my hands, well kept but workmanlike, not hands for a ring of such richness.

It would also be like wearing a label round my neck saying I was owned property. Rings can sound out strong signals.

'It's lovely.'

'That's not a no, is it? It doesn't sound like a yes.'

'It's too valuable.' Too large, too everything.

Over dinner, we talked first about me and my plans. I told Humphrey that I had received a flattering invitation to take part in the chief constables' course, but that I was doubtful. So I moved on to Billy Damiani. He was a hard man to discuss. I knew without being told that he kept all his secrets behind different doors and no one key opened the lot.

We were eating duck with orange. I have had periods of being a vegetarian but I think I am a carnivore at heart. Besides, it was wild duck, mallard, which is a superior creature to eat to the domesticated bird, being more flavoursome and less fatty. Humphrey had chosen the red wine to go with it and this too was good.

'May I have some water?' English hotels hate to give you water although they are very obliging with the bottled fizzy stuff which sometimes seems to cost as much as the wine. Mary Erskine was not there to cast magic over me, but Humphrey seemed to have an even more powerful aura. The waiter scuttled to bring me the water.

I was not, as it happens, wearing the ring, but it sat in its box on the table between us.

'Tell me what you know about Billy Damiani,' I said.

'I should guess you could find out anything you wanted to know for yourself.'

'Now come on, don't be difficult. What I want is your judgement on him and all those secret little details men like you always know about people.'

He drank some wine, considering what I had said. 'You can be sharp sometimes.'

'Yes, I know, it goes with the job,' I said impatiently. 'Come on. Why don't you want to talk about him?'

The red wine swirled round in his glass. 'The answer is I don't want to talk about him in relation to you. I don't like to think of him in relation to you. I wish he had not approached you. He shouldn't have done.'

'He's frightened, he thinks I can help. He's not interested in *me*.'

'You're wrong there. He thinks you're very sexy. Says so.'

'Well, damn him.' I sat back. 'And how do you know?'

He didn't answer that, but poured us some more wine. 'I should like to think he will be damned.' A streak of good old-fashioned Calvinism with its belief in hell and damnation showed itself in Humphrey on occasion. A dose of equally old-fashioned jealousy helped him along there this time. I was interested in that, too old to regard it as a trophy in the wars of sex, but interested.

'There's no evidence he killed Chloe Devon,' I said. 'But he might have done. He's certainly under suspicion.'

'I don't know anything about him that will be of any use to you in anything you want to do in this case.'

I shrugged. 'I'm not required to do anything, not my case. I'm just curious.'

'He is rich, the origin of the money is mysterious but is generally believed to have come from a small inheritance which he speculated with successfully. Property, anything that made money. That isn't an answer and it means we don't really know but there is a hint of some criminal connection. I think the money is real,' he said cautiously, 'however acquired, drugs possibly, but he is past master of the good-appearance game.'

'You hate him,' I said.

For a moment Humphrey did not answer, then he said: 'I believe I do.'

'It's not like you to be so personal.'

'Yes, it is. Life's personal. Sometimes I think you don't notice that.'

I looked at him over my wine glass. 'You really are angry with me. It's the ring, isn't it?'

'No, it's not. It's the whole thing. You are so bloody difficult to pin down.'

'And I thought you were.'

We were quarrelling and somehow Billy Damiani came into it. This quarrel was not totally my fault. I felt the anger of a person wrongly accused. And because I was angry, I didn't say anything, but sat there in silence.

My anger quietened down, and I found questions in

my mind. What was there between these two men and would I ever discover it? Or was it just one of those little masculine secrets that women find so hard to understand?

And was it possible that Humphrey was the reason that Damiani had come to me for help?

If it was help he had in mind and not some unidentifiable motive of his own.

I was seeing Humphrey in a new light, and my anger cooled still more. It didn't stop our quarrel exactly but it slowed it down.

'Coffee by the fire, sir?' said the obliging waiter.

As we stood up, I said to Humphrey: 'Just in case it clears your mind on anything I do not fancy Billy Damiani.'

As we walked towards the blazing fire by which a silver pot of coffee was waiting for us, I saw Thomas Dryden in the bar. He was drinking quietly and seriously by himself. And now he did not look like a farmer or a poet but like a man who drank for a profession. He made a gesture of recognition, something between a nod and bow. He knew who I was now, all of Brideswell knew, I was the 'woman police officer', and as such an object of interest and gossip to the whole village. I was beginning to understand by now that Brideswell was Byzantine in its relationships.

Humphrey picked up his coffee cup. 'Who's that?'

'Thomas Dryden, lives in the village, I don't know where.'

'He's putting it away a bit.'

I glanced towards Dryden. 'He's unhappy, I think.'

Humphrey gave him another look. 'Any special reason, or just general depression?'

'I don't know but I think it must be connected with the death of his wife.' I added: 'A lot of deaths recently in that family. No, don't look at me like that; nothing in my line of business, natural deaths.'

'Sure?'

'As far as I know.'

He raised an eyebrow. 'And you haven't asked any questions?'

He knew me too well. A series of deaths close together in one family always make me suspicious.

I had to admit that I had asked a few questions in the right quarters. 'All the deaths of the Beasleys seem to have been accepted as natural . . .' Illness, a viral infection of unknown origin for the Beasley family, or possibly poison if you believed Ellen Bean. There would have been an inquest but it must have returned a bland verdict. It might be worth discovering.

Only for Katherine Dryden who had died in a car crash had there been a faint suggestion of a query: an accident, she had taken a difficult bend too fast. So said the coroner's inquest and the local CID had accepted it. No problem.

But it was the sort of accident one could always wonder about.

As if he knew I was thinking about him, Thomas Dryden raised his head and gave me a smile. I smiled back. We didn't know each other except by sight but it looked as though that just might change soon.

The coffee was good, hot and strong. I could see why the Red Dragon prospered, the food and drink there was genuine and if the prices were high then you got what you paid for.

'A good-looking chap,' said Humphrey morosely. 'Or he would be when sober.'

I put down my coffee cup. 'Let's have a really good quarrel and get it over with.'

'I'm not quarrelling.'

'No, it takes two, I agree, as in other activities.' I waited for a laugh or at least a smile but none came. I hesitated. There was something here that needed healing and I must try to heal it. I stretched out a hand. He was wearing a nice greyish rough tweed which I had always

52

liked. 'Don't go back to London or wherever tonight.'

'It would be nice to miss the drive.'

'Miss it then.' I was thinking hard: I had coffee, bread, honey, and Cooper's Oxford Marmalade. There would be breakfast.

Through the open window, I saw a young policeman hurrying past. Perhaps he always hurried, but I was interested enough to go to the window and look out.

Something seemed to be going on down by the church. By leaning sideways I could see a car parked, a van with its headlights on, and several people standing by.

I went back to the fire. 'I think there may have been an accident. I'm going to take a look.'

Humphrey stood up. 'I'll come with you.'

As we got nearer to the church it became clear that the centre of interest was not in the churchyard but on the stretch of woodland beyond. Even as we looked I saw the vet's white van start up, headlights full on, and drive across the grass to the trees. A thicket of shrubs hid the heart of the wood.

A man standing underneath a tree was illuminated; he was holding a couple of terriers on a leash. He waved with his hand and pointed to the inner wood. I recognized Dr Harlow with his Jack Russells.

The van stopped, and still leaving the lights on, the vet leapt out to join Dr Harlow under the trees. They walked forward together. I walked faster towards the light and into the trees, not noticing if Humphrey was following or not. The constable got there before I did.

Dr Harlow and Tim Abbey were staring down at something under a big oak. One of the dogs was whining. Without saying a word, the young vet took the leash and led the dogs to the van, put them in, and shut the door. I could hear the whining and scratching as I walked past.

The lights of the van penetrated the belt of leaves and shone on the grass under the tree, shone on the earth where it had been turned over by the dogs as they had scrabbled. I saw Ellen Bean and her husband walking across from the road, leaning forward, faces keen and sharp.

Where the strong light hit it the earth under the trees was very brown and the grass a very bright green. I could see something sticking out of the earth. The soil lay lightly upon it but I could make out a humpy shape.

I walked over to look. The dogs had dug up the upper part of a human torso. There was no head, but we had the ribcage. We had the heart.

FIVE

I was late back to the house that night, as men from the Southern CID swarmed in to set up a centre in the village. The rain had stopped, it was quiet night with a full moon. I was conscious as I walked through the village of curtains pulled aside, of curious faces behind the windows.

I was on my own. I had not noticed at what point Humphrey went away. The BMW was gone from outside the front door, but someone had made up the fire so that it still blazed. This act from Humphrey, because it could be no one else, showed kindness and thought. But there was nothing else. No note, nothing. I poured a drink and sat by the fire considering the events of the night.

Granted that we had no head, and assuming we had the remains of Chloe Devon, the Met would have to yield jurisdiction. By tradition, whoever has the heart gets the rest of the body.

I did not know who would be working the case, but Clive Barney, a detective chief superintendent whom I had met, had arrived so he would probably keep control. I knew about him, of course, it was my job to know. He had had a good career, with quick promotions, and was said to be liked. His most notable case had been the last, a triple murder in the railway station at Slocombe Regis. He had got to the killer quickly, not difficult perhaps as the man had left an envelope with his name and address on it at the scene of the killing, but there had been some questions asked about the rough handling of the killer when in custody. The man had hanged himself. The general opinion had been that Barney would go far if he didn't shoot his own foot off first.

Muff arrived to sit by the fire and consider life with me. Her coat was damp, so I guessed it must now be raining. I didn't envy the police team still working in the wood where the body had been found. Muff rubbed against me transferring some of the wetness to my left leg. The matter of the mouse was not raised. She was just one of the creatures with sharp teeth in the village, some domestic, some wild: dogs, rats, ferrets, and squirrels.

Barney had his supporters with him, Inspector Church and Sergeant Mary Elchie, whom I knew. They were a part of a new Violent Crimes Unit which had been put together in some hurry from a number of different area CID squads. It was new, as yet untried, and said to have loyalty problems. They were just names but I fancied I had heard of Elchie as being a rising star. She was a sturdy young woman, not pretty but almost handsome. All three treated me warily; I was aware that they would have preferred me not to be around.

But I had been there, on the spot from the beginning, and I could not be ignored. My position as someone who knew everything, who had to be told everything (even if on microfilm or discs) made me important. The newly acquired investigatory arm made me dangerous. A threat.

I sipped my drink. I knew that was how they reasoned, and to a certain extent it was true. I didn't intend to be a threat to anyone, but I did poke around. I was licensed to poke around.

It isn't human nature to like that, and most certainly not police nature.

I had not told them that I knew Billy Damiani but I would have to do so and soon, before they found out for themselves. They would not like me any better for knowing him.

56

The drink tasted sour on my tongue, so I put it aside and took myself out into the kitchen to make some tea. Muff looked at me, considered following and decided against. It was cold in the kitchen and smelt damp. I would have to do something about it.

I took the tea back before the fire, kicked off my shoes, and crouched before the flames. It was a wood fire, smoky and deliciously scented with apple, but I was having some unpleasing thoughts.

When bits of Chloe Devon had started turning up all over London, then it had looked as if she had been killed in London. That she had somehow got back to the big city and been killed there.

Now it looked as if she had never got far from Brideswell after all. So where did that leave Billy Damiani?

He was in trouble in any case and would certainly come in for more questioning; I could see the line the questions would take.

Chloe Devon had left the Red Dragon on her own, she had been seen leaving, she had not been seen after that moment. Billy Damiani had waited for some time, half an hour so he had said, and then driven back to London. Had he met her on the road and picked her up?

That was the question I would be asking. It would be interesting to see how he handled it. If I knew Billy Damiani he would already be calling his lawyers.

Thoughts of Damiani brought my mind back to Humphrey, whereupon guilt flooded in at once. Guilt and then anger, because he had left me silently, hadn't he, and marched off without a word? It was almost rage; I sat there relishing the rage for a moment.

But I couldn't keep up the anger and the guilt surged back. My fault, usually my fault. I did distance myself and maybe I had done it once too often this time. I drank the tea with a miserable sick feeling. Muff came up and rubbed her head against me, offering comfort and at the same time marking me as her property.

The doorbell rang. I sat listening, then it rang again. I got up to open it, removing Muff from my foot. Two tall figures sheltering under one umbrella stood there.

'Crick, David. Come in.'

They hesitated, a polite pair as always. 'Not too late, is it?'

I held the door open wider. Muff took her chance to escape, a small fleeting figure, tail waving. 'Damn. Come in, you two.'

'She'll come back,' said David.

'I always worry.'

'I've seen her all over the village, she knows her way around . . . We had to come.'

'I'm all right,' I said, in surprise. Was this someone else trying to look after me?

'Of course, It's us that are all shook up . . . It was the girl, Chloe Devon?'

'Can't be sure. Probably.' I didn't want to talk about it to them. 'I won't be directly concerned, you know.' Unless I wanted to be, and no need to tell them that fact. 'I'm drinking tea, would you like some?'

'Love some,' said David. 'Shall I get mugs from the kitchen?'

I nodded. 'You know where they are.' Not clean though, I thought, domesticity had taken a back seat lately.

Crick looked around the room. 'Your man not here?'

'He had to go off.' I could hear David sloshing water round the mugs. I grinned at him as he came back in.

Crick nodded. 'Nice car he's got.' The two men kept a very ancient and much loved Citroën. Crick said he had an aesthetic identity with it. The car certainly had an antique elegance. 'Saw it had gone.'

Of course you did, I thought, the village watched everything. Which made the way Chloe Devon had never been observed in that walk down the village street even more incredible.

Someone had seen her. Probably more than one village pair of eyes.

'Does begin to look as if she never got away from the village.'

I nodded, wondering what they had really come calling for.

'So I suppose questions will be asked?'

'Yes,' I said, keeping my voice neutral. 'That will happen.' Feet up and down the village street, a knocking on doors.

'I kind of hate saying what we're going to say . . . It's why we came to you.'

My expression began bleak. 'I don't do favours.'

'Not looking for one. But you could tell us what we ought to do . . . Thing is, that night the girl disappeared, well, it's true enough, we didn't see her. But Harlow was out walking those dogs, all right, we can't suspect the Doc, and he says he didn't see her.' He gave me an opaque look. And that means you think he did, I said to myself. 'But Dryden was sitting on that bench in the churchyard for a long while . . . He ought to have seen something of her.'

'I've seen him there myself. He spends a lot of time in the churchyard.'

David said: 'Only since his wife died.'

'Yes, what exactly happened there?'

'What I've heard—' began David.

'You can't trust village gossip,' said Crick, 'we don't really know.'

'I know it must be connected with the deaths of the Beasley family,' I said.

'The story that went round was that Mrs Dryden brought home a wicked virus from the hospital where she worked, she had natural immunity but she was a carrier to this bug which killed off all the Beasley family.' He took a deep breath. 'And then she killed herself, accidentally on purpose in a car crash.'

59

It was more or less the story Ellen had told me, except she had hinted that she had brought in the idea of poison and that Dryden bore some responsibility for his wife's death, so it was certainly the accepted village tale.

'There must have been an inquest.'

'I expect there was one, but I don't know.'

I shrugged. 'It explains Dryden haunting the church-yard, I suppose, and if he was preoccupied, then it explains why he didn't see Chloe Devon.'

'Says he wasn't there,' said Crick. 'But he was. Thought we ought to say. Bit of a womanizer.'

'Not the only one in the village you could say that of,' said David. 'I mean look at Geoff Harlow, lovely chap but not exactly a one-woman man.'

'We don't know why the girl was killed. Sex may not come into it.'

'Do you have to have a motive?'

'One of some sort is usual,' I said drily. 'Unless mad-ness is involved. It doesn't have to be much sometimes, but a reason is needed.'

'Dryden attacked a man once when he was drunk. For making a comment about him sitting in the churchyard.' David looked ashamed. 'Me, actually.'

'Well, when asked you can tell the CID man who calls.'

'He will call?'

'I'll tell him to do that, shall I?'

'I don't like passing it on.'

'She was a nice kid,' said David sadly.

I was surprised. 'Did you know Chloe?'

'Not well, and not here. Met her in Rome, at a party at the British School. She was working there.'

And that, I thought, is the real reason you came here tonight. But knowing her is not a cause for suspicion in itself, and Billy Damiani certainly knew her better than I guess you did. At the moment he is the one doing the worrying.

'I shouldn't be too concerned about Dryden,' I said.

'Just say what you know and leave speculation out of it.'

'Right,' said Crick with relief. He gave David a quick look. 'We ought to be off. Mustn't keep you up.'

David stood up politely. 'It's always been a welcoming house.'

'It is a happy house,' I said. 'I wish I'd known Mrs Armitage. Mary Erskine tells me you knew her of old, Crick?'

'So I did, so I did. A lovely lady.'

I saw them to the door. As they departed, Muff rushed in, her coat wet again.

'Told you she'd be back,' they said with one voice.

I dried Muff, and carried her upstairs.

On the middle of the bed was the sapphire ring. A declaration, I thought, if I ever saw one.

SIX

I set my own operation in action the next morning.

I telephoned my assistant, George Rewley, formerly sergeant and newly promoted to inspector, who had just joined the Independent Investigation Unit, which we called the IU, and which local wags called the IOU, because we were always demanding information but not trading much back.

George Rewley was a good officer. He was sensitive, intelligent, and ambitious. He worked hard and with perception, closing some tough cases. I won't name them or describe them, that's like writing about Sherlock Holmes, isn't it? (Dr Watson: 'How well I remember the Case of the Strangled Strangers which Holmes had just completed so successfully, when we were plunged into another mystery . . .' and so on.)

Rewley had also had the good sense to marry a girl I was very fond of.

In addition, he had a rare skill. He could lip-read. The only member of his family with normal hearing, since his parents and his sibling lip-read then so did he. In certain cases this had been extremely useful. It also created a certain awe among his colleagues. Yes, he was a useful man. People came and went in my professional life: you chose them to work with you, or they were wished on you (not so often with me these days), you trained them in your ways, then they got promotion and moved on. I hoped Rewley would stay.

I interrupted him at his breakfast. I could hear the clink of china and the sound of the early morning news on the radio. 'Sorry, I want some information.'

I told him to talk to Billy Damiani, question him more closely about the quarrel with Chloe. Then to talk with the girl's friends, to get what he could on her background. It might be that her death was a chance affair, that she had wandered into the ambit of a killer and died because of it. But it might that the cause of her death lay in her own life. I wanted to know more about that life.

Find out about her stay in Italy, I instructed. Billy Damiani and her meeting with Crick and David in Rome did not a summer make, but I thought her past would bear looking into. Rewley had muttered something about this keeping him busy for some days.

I knew that Chief Superintendent Clive Barney was the type to keep his nose to the ground, scrupulous in his attention to the physical details, like the forensic evidence and the times and movements of parties concerned, but not likely to lift his imagination far beyond the present. And I did not think this was a case for doing just that.

I could trust Barney to worry around and about Dr Harlow, if indeed there was anything to worry about. He'd be doing that anyway: Harlow had found the headless trunk of Chloe Devon and the finder always aroused suspicion. Harlow would come in for scrutiny.

I would get all the straightforward reports that went through the normal channels, but I could take a look at other areas.

I was walking in where I was not wanted, but I had been doing that almost all my working life and I knew I could face out Clive Barney. He might be in trouble himself for the Slocombe Regis case and it was possible I could help him there.

Just for a second the picture of the man I had killed flashed into my mind. Crumpled, broken, bloody. Well, he had killed himself, but it had been my mind, my spirit, that had forced him to open the window and jump. I had got a confession out of him and he couldn't face himself or his punishment. He had looked at me as he jumped.

I made myself some coffee, a rich dark brew, and considered other matters closer home. I had a few personal thoughts to clear in my mind.

I hadn't slept well, too much adrenalin pumping round the system, and it wasn't only the discovery in the wood.

It was the matter of the ring. Left behind by the donor who had gone off without a word. I'm not sure if I could forgive that. But perhaps it was myself I could not forgive; I had forgotten Humphrey last night, absorbed in the unfolding drama beneath the trees by the church.

I tried to remember what had happened between us. I thought I had said something like 'Give me a few minutes,' but I could not remember what Humphrey had replied. Perhaps he hadn't said anything. Had he even been there with me under the trees?

The fact that I could not remember reproached me.

I drank some coffee, deep in thought. Kate did not like my relationship with Humphrey. It was not her business, she had made enough bad choices herself in the past, and I hadn't asked for her judgement, but that did not stop Kate.

'He's not right for you,' she had said, 'he's too safe.' She had sought for a word. 'He's too constricting . . . You always get hitched up with that sort of man.'

I wasn't quite clear what sort of a man Kate thought I needed, but I was aware that Kate never made a play for safety. If there was a risky choice, she took it. Her marriage had to be put in that category. It might go either way, and I suspected that Rewley knew it. I also knew that he was man enough to match Kate.

Time to dress, a working day stretched ahead. I looked at my diary: a late morning committee in London, then a meeting back in the Berkshire HQ, that was just the skeleton, plenty more would have to be done.

Hanging on a hook in the bathroom was the dress I had taken off last night, there was mud on the hem of the black corded silk. The shoes, from Ferragamo, had dark earth and grass plastered all over them. They would clean but I was doubtful about my suede shoulder bag which seemed to have met some dark sticky something that I trusted was not blood.

I dressed quickly, did a brisk tidying-up operation in the bedroom, bathroom, and kitchen, then I filled Muff's food and water bowl, left her litter tray immaculate, and checked where she was.

No sign of her. Somehow she had managed to get out; I remembered now that I had opened the kitchen window briefly to see if it was still raining, and by the time I had settled that to my satisfaction and shut it again, she must have taken her chance to slip through. She was adept at that trick. I didn't always see her go, the invisible flash-past-me cat. I didn't like to leave for the day without knowing where she was.

I grabbed my top coat because it was cold if not wet and walked out into the village to look for her.

For a moment I hesitated about which way to go, but then I decided to walk towards the church. I was not averse to this stroll down the main street. There was a grim dialogue going on in this village and I ought to listen to it.

I walked down the street very slowly, looking about me for the cat. I didn't call her name, there was no need. If she saw me she would show herself to me, as she always did. Lines of parked cars and a long coach showed me that the police had moved in to establish an Incident Room. As I got closer a trail of cables stretching from a manhole to the coach showed that they had their electronic equipment in place. Overnight they had worked fast.

Outside the baker's shop, which I now recognized as a central meeting place for the village since it also housed the Post Office, a small line had formed. I put myself behind a tall blonde girl with big blue eyes. She wore jeans, a sweater, a friendly smile, and she had the pale fairness of the Scandinavian.

'You from Sweden?'

'Yes, I am working with Tim, with the animals. I am Lu, short for Louise. We had a Queen Louise, you know. I think she was English.'

'Ah yes.' I nodded, the queue was moving slowly forward. 'Do you like the work?'

'He is a lovely man, so kind, and I love him and he loves me. He has little rages but I take no notice. All men have moods, there is a little demon in all of them. I say be a good boy or I will beat you.'

'And do you?'

'No, because he would like it too much.' She giggled. 'And that is not good, I think. He falls down a black hole sometimes.'

She obviously believed in total confession.

'He is so generous, he say to me you should be draped in pale mink. I will give you mink. I say to him but no one wears mink now, it is cruel, and he was surprised.' She laughed. 'Perhaps he will grow me some diamonds.' She saw my face. 'That is a joke,' she explained carefully.

Behind me I heard Ellen Bean give a snort. 'Silly girl,' she said.

I could see the look on her face that meant village gossip was coming. 'She doesn't know him like I do. If there's a bigger womanizer in the village than the doctor, then it's him. Once you could rely on the vicar and the doctor and the vet to pay their bills. I say nothing about the parson, he does the best he can.'

'Debts?' I said.

'There's a recession on you, you know. Mortgaged and borrowed to the hilt, the lot of them.'

Then she turned to the woman behind her, a slender woman with well-dressed grey hair. She was wearing jeans

66

and a sweater, and looked every inch the actress. I hardly needed Ellen to introduce me to Nora Garden.

'Nora, this is my friend Charmian Daniels.' Ellen seemed to take a dour pleasure in knowing me.

Nora Garden smiled and held out a well-manicured hand. 'Oh, lovely, but I've heard of you. You've had a lot of media attention.'

More than I wanted, I thought, and wondered what stories she had picked up. Some I would rather have had buried.

As I left with my purchases, Muff materialized on a garden wall behind me. 'Oh, there you are.' With relief I stretched out my hands to pick her up. Muff looked at me, studied the other two women, then effortlessly jumped into Ellen's grasp.

'That's a proper witches' cat,' said Ellen with approval as Muff stared, calm and complacent, from her arms.

'She's my cat,' I was hurt. 'Very much my cat.'

'Mine if I want her,' said Ellen.

I was about to protest when I remembered the many hours that Muff spent with Winifred Eagle and Bridie Peacock, witches emeritus. It was likely that Muff had picked up a tip or two. Looking at her now, I could believe it.

'No witchcraft, please,' I said.

'I retired when I married.'

'Bean is a very good witch's name,' said Nora Garden, aligning herself unmistakably on my side in this war that seemed to be going on.

As we stood there, we all saw a car draw up and first a man I recognized as Clive Barney got out and then Dr Harlow.

Ellen said gleefully: 'Dr Harlow, eh? Wonder what trouble he's got buried in his backyard?'

'You sound as if you don't like the doctor?'

Nora Garden smiled. 'Naturally Ellen doesn't like doctors, she does her own healing.'

I reclaimed my cat. 'I must take this creature back.'

'Let her get home on her own,' said Ellen, turning away. She was going towards the police encampment. 'I suppose you know everything that's going on in there?' She nodded her head towards it.

I didn't answer. If I had been honest I would have said: 'Not as much as I would like.' It was automatic among certain of my colleagues to guard the left hand from knowing what the right hand was doing. And if on the left was a woman, well, all their instincts were to stay on guard.

Muff began to struggle so that I dropped the keys to the house. 'Damn.'

Nora Garden picked them up, moving in one elegant liquid movement that I envied. I am fit and reasonably athletic, but she moved beautifully. I wondered if she had ever been a dancer.

'I'll help you,' she said. 'Be glad to. You have a happy house. I loved Beatrice Armitage.'

'I wish I'd known her.'

'Not easy. Layers to Beatrice. I never called her Bea, by the way. Beatrice is such a lovely name.'

'She called herself Duchess sometimes, I've been told.'

'Sometimes, sometimes. Just a joke.' She unlocked my front door and held it open for me.

Muff and I entered, and I let Muff go, she stalked off, pride injured.

'Come in, it's a muddle, but I shall get it in order . . . I'm afraid it's changed from what you knew,' I said, seeing her look around.

'Oh, things have to change. Beatrice would have been the first to say so.'

There was still some coffee left, so we went into the kitchen and sat drinking it. As we drank I studied my companion.

I had known Nora Garden by reputation for some years; I had seen her on the television screen and on the stage in various parts, some tragic, some comic. She was better at light comedy. She was not a star but she worked steadily which was more than most players can say. As far as I knew she had never married, but she had the air of a happy woman. And did I say she was slim, and beautifully dressed? Nothing helps a woman more. Jeans she may have been wearing, but they were of soft suede and the sweater was cashmere.

'I'll have to redecorate,' I said apologetically.

'She lived like a great lady to the end, except of course right at the end when she was a bit incapacitated, but we all deteriorate at last, don't we?' said Nora sadly. 'But there wasn't a lot of money left by that time, if there ever had been much. She was so generous, lent money, gave money away.' She shook her head. 'It didn't mean much to her. I had started to bully her a bit about that.'

I wondered if Mary Erskine had borrowed from her aunt? Mary was always hard up, and although she had scruples, they were not always the ones you expected.

'Tell me more.'

'You never saw her? She never was a great beauty but she had so much charm, so much goodness, that was her secret. And she always married for love. Money never came into it. She couldn't resist a beautiful face.'

'Quite a few in the village,' I said, thinking of some of the faces of the men I had seen.

Nora laughed. 'Aren't there? I've noticed myself, unusually high number. And I'm sure Beatrice appreciated everyone.' Nora put down her mug. It was mugs that day, no good china had migrated from Windsor yet. 'You make better coffee than Beatrice ever did. Couldn't cook, of course. Her generation, her class, never did.' She laughed. 'She served you the most terrible food on cracked plates, she never minded about that either, but she did it with such an air.'

I could believe what she said, the state of the kitchen suggested it. Persian rugs on the floor, perhaps even a picture or two, but the oldest cooker I had ever seen.

'I thought she'd live for ever. I was surprised when she died. I was on tour and by the time I got back to Brideswell, she was dead. She took ill, lingered for a few days but never came back to life.' Nora put her beautiful hands together as if in benediction. 'Poor love. God, I miss her.'

'Had you known her long?'

'Only since I came to the village . . . But you could say I came because of her. My grandfather worked for her father. As gardener. So I'd always known about her. The marriages and the gossip. She was a sort of symbol of glamour to me. Someone to learn from.'

I thought Nora was glamorous herself. No longer young, but by no means old, there was a sort of shine to her. If she had learnt that from Beatrice Armitage, then Lady Mary's Aunt Bee had been quite something.

'And she used to send telegrams when I had a First Night, come and sit in the stalls and clap. Never came to the dressing room, though. But I'd send a thank-you card and she'd a card at Christmas. I suppose I came to live here because I wanted to know her better.'

And why did you come? her eyes said.

She got her answer. 'Lady Mary is a friend of mine. She showed me the house. I'm looking forward to living here.'

'But you will still work in Windsor?' Her eyes were bright with interest.

'My base. But I mean to be here a lot.'

'I'm here when I'm not working. Wasn't at home when that poor girl disappeared.'

I wasn't willing to talk about that, although I was interested that she had wanted me to know that fact, but I probed at an area that interested me. 'Did you know the Beasley family?'

'The ones who died, those three?' She shook her head. 'That was tragic, a whole family wiped out like that, and then Kath Dryden going. There are other Beasleys,

70

Drydens too for that matter, all over the place. Two of the old village families. No, I was filming when they died, I didn't know them except by sight. I suppose we said good morning and what a nice day, but that was about it. The old villagers tend to keep themselves to themselves, as they would put it. Newcomers are treated politely but not like real villagers. Except for the Cremornes who fit in. Well, the family owns most of the place still. You've met David and Crick, I suppose?'

I nodded.

'Have you read his book? Brilliant, I believe, he's a natural scholar. No money there either, Crick's got a small pension, David has just what he earns from writing, and he always says not much. They are lucky to live in that house, rent free.'

'He could get a job, I suppose.'

'Don't know what as. He's a real scholar and they're usually unemployable.'

Unemployable. I added the word to my picture of David. Perhaps Nora didn't like him very much. I was learning about the complicated relationships in Brideswell.

She sighed. 'I'd better go. I was on my way to buy a loaf.' And collect all the gossip of the day. She could still do that. 'Thanks for the coffee.'

At the door, she paused. 'You know, this house is haunted. Beatrice is still here, perhaps she always will be. But she must like you. The house still feels happy.' She kissed my cheek very lightly. 'Bless you, dear.'

And with a flourish of her cashmere throw, she was gone. Muff had gone too.

Later that day I found out what had been found hidden in Dr Harlow's backyard: he had Chloe's head.

SEVEN

There was a ghost in Brideswell, one in my own house, so Nora Garden said, but I had yet to see its face.

Its face? Is it neuter or do ghosts have a sex? Surely this one, if it existed at all, always a matter for doubt, had a sex? Both sexes. It had a man-woman face. A face that opened its mouth, with a tongue that wailed and whipped.

This was how I saw it later.

At this time all I knew was that two people, Ellen Bean and Nora Garden had spoken of this ghost to me. The two women knew each other so perhaps it was the same ghost. But I was not sure that they were truly friends.

As I got myself ready to leave for the day after Nora had left (I was going to be late), I knew I did not believe in ghosts. Nora had implied that Beatrice was the ghost, possibly a happy haunter and this house her ground; Ellen's ghost sounded a different character altogether and not nearly so nice to know.

Later, I was to feel the force of this spirit.

Of course, Ellen Bean, as I was to realize, would not have been interested in a happy ghost, only one raw and hungry would have caught her attention. She had met such a lost soul before, no doubt, and recognized Brideswell's affliction for what it was. I ought to have trusted Ellen's senses, she knew what she'd got.

I left a window in the kitchen open a few inches for Muff to return. Unwise, perhaps, but I did not expect to be robbed with so many police in the village. I expected they would be keeping a quiet surveillance on my house in any case. I was an object of interest to them quite apart from the murder. I had heard that there was a rumour going around that I was retiring to grow roses.

I walked round the kitchen, checking all was in order and as safe as I could leave it. No smouldering matches, no kettle left plugged in. I had been ironing my skirt: the iron was cold.

I observed once again the mark on the wall by the Aga. There was a hook and mark as if something had once hung there.

I put my hand on it, the wall was cold, cold. That's my ghost, I said aloud.

Outside, standing by my car, I stopped myself. There is always something you don't know, a voice inside me said. There is always something you don't know.

Question to ask Ellen Bean: When did your ghost die?

EIGHT

As soon as I walked into my office I studied a fax that had just arrived.

It told me where the doctor had found Chloe's head. Or rather, he had not found it, it had been found for him. Not by his dogs, as might have been expected, but by the police.

The head, minus most of the hair, which had been cut off, had been found in the compost heap at the bottom of his garden. An intensive search of the whole area by the police had turned it up.

Perhaps they had been concentrating on his garden since he had found the torso, but only they knew and they were not saying. Just a routine search, had been the line.

Educated, sophisticated men, who might be killers do not bury the head of the victim in their own backyard. Or do they?

Plainly Chief Superintendent Barney found this a very perplexing question. He did not want to believe it of the doctor. But I knew the questions he would be asking Harlow.

Did you know the dead girl?

Had you ever seen her?

Have you any explanation of how her head was found behind the shed in your garden?

It would be gently and politely done, because Harlow was a doctor and a gentleman, a respectable figure.

74

What I did not know, not being party to their private thinking, was whether the investigating team really considered the doctor a suspect or whether they were playing by the rules.

And then it would be their turn to have a go at Billy Damiani, taking over from the Met squad (who would certainly still be in the background). They would be putting their own version of the questions that had already been asked of him. The questioning would be sharper and tougher now that it looked as if Chloe had never left the village alive.

Damiani wouldn't like it, and surely this was why he had tried to involve me, so that he would have a protective barrier. I was meant to be that screen.

I didn't know what Clive Barney and his team thought of Billy, or his involvement in the murder, I didn't know what I thought myself. But I did know he was a prime manipulator and had tried to manipulate me.

That made me suspicious. People like Billy Damiani, sharp as they were, had their own stupidities, and he had been stupid about me. No doubt he often underrated women. He had certainly underrated me if he thought I would in any manner dance to his tune, and it might very well be that he had underrated Lady Mary Dalmeny Erskine. She would keep her distance now if Billy was seriously suspected of murder.

I met Lady Mary as I took a brief trip to Maid of Honour Row midmorning. The rush of paperwork was over, and I wanted to see what was going on in my house, if anything, and collect some more clothes.

She was putting an envelope through my letter box. She looked at me in surprise. 'Didn't expect to see you.' She withdrew the envelope. 'Your office said you had gone to London.'

'I shall be going later. What's that?'

'Your copy of the lease for the house. If you still want

to buy, we can go ahead when the will is through probate.'

'Certainly I want to buy, I am quite settled on it. You know that.'

'Things change sometimes,' said Lady Mary. 'I've seen Humphrey. He doesn't seem very happy. I don't think he likes the idea of that house.'

'He'll get used to it.'

'You really are rough.'

I was silent. Humphrey could fight his own battles. I wasn't going to ask her how and where she had spoken to Humphrey. They had met somewhere, they moved in the same circles. I knew there was a link between them that I should have to learn to live with. She claimed she was looking after his rose garden.

'And then there's the murder. He doesn't care for that either. Of course, I know that wouldn't put you off. It's your way of life, after all.'

'Thanks.'

'Well, I didn't mean it quite that way.' She did, though, just a little bit, she had shown a claw and now retracted it. Strangely enough, Mary's little scratches endeared her to me rather than otherwise, they defined her. Defined me too, I suppose, in my reaction to her.

She was a mixture of childlike emotion and social sophistication. So like her the trip to Paris with Damiani. I shook my head at her and laughed.

'Liar. Of course, you did.'

'Oh well, I have to be forgiven. I'm in misery about my young man and it makes me evil.'

'Where is he?'

She shrugged. 'Somewhere dangerous.'

I knew that her beloved specialized in bombs and their violent behaviour. She was probably right to be miserable.

'I heard about the find in the village . . . It is Chloe Devon?'

'Yes.' She did not, of course, yet know about the find-

76

ing of the head. This had not yet been formally identified but it fitted her description, and the knife marks on the base of the neck matched those on the torso. There were not two bodies. It seemed there were other marks too, bite marks as on the hand which had been found in south London. 'Did you know her?'

She shook her head. 'No, thank goodness. Saw her in the distance once with Billy.' She added: 'Did he do it, do you think?'

I shrugged. 'No idea.'

'He's quite frightening sometimes, cold, hard. But I don't think he'd kill in that way.'

I was inclined to believe her. Billy would hire a killer.

'And why should he?'

'Oh, motive. Sometimes you only establish the motive at the end, sometimes never.'

But Mary was following her own thoughts through. 'If Billy did kill her, then it wouldn't be sex, not even money. Be position. If she threatened that in some way, then he might.'

'Position?'

'Status, social position, you know. Who asked him to dinner, where he could visit, the parties and private views he was asked to.'

The snob killing, I thought.

'Bea met him once, I introduced him, and she said: "Only a second-rate scoundrel." '

'So he was in the house?' Somehow, I didn't like that thought.

'Oh, yes, in fact, he thought of buying the house himself.'

'After Mrs Armitage died?'

'That's how he met Chloe. She showed him round. She worked for Astley Green, the estate agents. He liked her and offered her a job.'

I had the feeling that I was hearing something important.

'Thanks for mentioning it,' I said. 'Can I give you a lift? I'm just off.'

'No, my car is round the corner. See you.' She gave me a sad smile and a little wave. She had that wave to perfection.

Lady Mary in sorrow, I thought cynically, as I watched her walk away. I let her go, then checked my house. Repairs were under way but by no means complete. Not a workman to be seen, of course.

I drove to London for my meeting, but my deeper thoughts remained in Windsor.

I had sent Rewley out to investigate Billy Damiani, and I thought he could handle it. However Barney reacted, I could leave it there and return to other duties. One of these duties was to run an assessing eye over any case which seemed to hang fire, not to be coming to a satisfactory conclusion. Since all information came into my office sooner or later, I was in a position to give an overall judgement.

That was the theory at least. But since all CID units were past masters at keeping what they wanted to themselves, I had to be sharp-eyed and suspicious. Nature had equipped me well for just that function and I had developed a kind of sense of when I was being fogged.

What I did not expect was that the case involving Chief Superintendent Barney and the suspect in the triple killing should be such a case.

In Slocombe Regis, which boarded Slough, and which had once been a small village and was now a sprawling industrial estate, three people had been shot dead in the waiting room at the railway station. It was not a regular stop, it was known as Slocombe Halt, and carried no staff. A grubby, dusty windswept spot in which to die. After the shooting of the three men, all of whom were his friends, Michael Finnucane had gone drinking, been arrested for causing a brawl, and had then confessed to murder.

Slocombe Regis might not have a proper railway stop but it had its own police station to which Finnucane was taken. It was quite by chance that Chief Superintendent Barney had been on the spot, since he would not have been involved in this apparently straightforward murder. He had been visiting an old mate. He had taken over, questioned Finnucane, who had then made his confession, and that had tidied things up nicely.

He had then hanged himself in his cell. Next day, it had been discovered he had no gun and had the mental age of seven.

Not so tidy.

So I was now in contact with Clive Barney on two fronts. I would need to use some tact. My friends said that tact was not what I was good at, my enemies put it even stronger.

Tired and still preoccupied, I returned in the late afternoon to my office.

I checked all calls and messages. Nothing as yet from George Rewley.

My secretary said goodbye and departed. 'I've left you a pot of coffee,' she said. 'Drink it while it's fresh.'

'Will do.' She did her best to mother me, which was ridiculous since I was older than she was. But she meant well, so I would humour her and drink the coffee.

With some impatience, I was waiting for Rewley to report. I felt restless, tired and yet unable to relax. So I worked away at papers, made several telephone calls, and studied the tapes of the interviews with the hanged man. It didn't seem to me that Clive Barney had pressurized him. I stayed late at my desk, hoping Rewley would call.

I was on the point of going off, driving back to Brideswell, when he telephoned. He had a good telephone manner.

'Do you want to take this call or shall I send in a report? I've got plenty to say.'

'I want to hear.'

He did not need to consult notes, although I guessed he had several careful pages; Rewley did not forget details.

'It took me some time to get what I wanted. No one wanted to talk about Chloe Devon. I think Damiani must have got there before me with a warning . . . I found out some things about him, too.'

'Good.'

'I'm not saying anything I have will solve the case, but it's interesting. To begin with, Chloe Devon had not been working for Damiani for long. Before that she had a job with a big Knightsbridge estate agent, Astley Green, you know them, I expect. She was selling for them. She didn't stay long there but moved to another firm, I haven't got the name of that as yet. But you may have heard of Astley Green?'

'I've come across them.'

'It was how she met Damiani. I got that from one of the girls in the *Arian* office, tell you about that later. And I went along to Lowndes Square where Astley Green have their office.' He paused. 'Smart place.'

I had gone there once in the way of business, tracking down a swindler with a taste for smart rented apartments. I could remember the office with its soft thick carpet, the pale polished-wood desks, the pretty young women, with the view of a distinguished-looking grey-haired man in an inner room. The image was carefully constructed: expense personified.

'I had to make myself felt,' said Rewley thoughtfully.

I nodded. I could imagine the impact of Rewley's arrival, tall, quiet of voice, but so clearly not a buyer, nor a seller, but a policeman.

'They don't like the police dropping in, scares off some of their trade.' Arabs, Lebanese, rich world-commuters, millionaire gypsies, these were the sort on whom Astley Green prospered.

'One or two of the girls remembered Chloe Devon.

The turnover of young female staff is high there. Most of the girls get married, or just move on.'

'As Chloe did.'

'As she did. But while there she got the reputation of being a hard worker. She was good at selling and seemed to enjoy it. She might have moved up the ladder fast, but she met Damiani and he took a fancy to her and lured her away.'

'Is that what was said?'

'It was the implication, but to be fair, fine art was her chief interest, she'd been working in Rome.' He paused. 'In the Astley Green office I managed to talk to one of the girls, Susie Marker, who had known Chloe a bit better than most. She let me take her out and give her a cup of coffee. She said that something happened to Chloe when she went to the house in Brideswell to show Damiani round . . . An episode, she called it.'

'With him?'

'Not necessarily, just something that intrigued her . . . It's your house, by the way.'

'So I've heard.'

There was a coffee house near to Astley Green's, I'd stopped in it myself, the coffee was good and hot. I remembered a warm brioche and cherry jam. It was always crowded with theatre people because it was near a casting agency. Rewley must have marked it down as a good spot for a meeting on his way past.

Already I had learnt bits of the story Rewley was unfolding. I knew Chloe had met Damiani in my house. I could imagine her waiting for him, walking up and down to keep the cold out, and then seeing him drive up in that big car.

Of course, that picture might be quite wrong, and they might have driven down together.

'Are you sure the episode had anything to do with Damiani?'

'Susie did not know, but she thought not. Chloe did go to work for him shortly afterwards.'

81

Susie could be wrong.

'I think I got all I could out of Susie. Nice kid. None of the people I was talking to there knew Damiani, he had no contact with them except for that one time he wanted to view the house in Brideswell. He never made a serious offer, and never came back. After leaving Susie, I went back to the *Arian* office. I'd made an arrangement to give one of the girls there a drink.' He paused.

Rewley was good-looking and dressed well; he wouldn't have found it hard to engage the interest of the girls.

'There's a wine bar next to the *Arian* offices and we went there. One of those dark little places like being inside a leather box. Dark red leather in this case and probably plastic. I was right, this girl Deborah, with the rest of them, had been told by Damiani to watch her tongue if anyone asked questions, but she's leaving anyway. She's a serious art historian, says he isn't, doesn't know a Picasso from a Giotto. The magazine loses money, of course, and she thinks he might be getting fed up with it. Or even getting short of money.' Rewley laughed. 'I think she hopes it is that. You can see she doesn't rate him, she says people like him upset the art market.'

I knew *Arian*, it was a beautifully produced magazine on lovely thick paper, the illustrations to the articles were of very high quality, while the articles themselves were the work of important scholars. It was a useful showpiece for the art world and would be missed.

'Damiani subsidizes it for social reasons. They are both social climbers but at least the sister knows more what she's doing in the art world. So Deborah says. And he's a womanizer.'

He had come to his main point.

'Worked through the office, as far as he could that is, not everyone took him on, Deborah says she didn't, but he liked to pursue. Could turn nasty. Lately, he's been a bit quieter, not getting out to so many smart parties. She thinks he's got problems.'

Chief Superintendent Barney would certainly have picked that fact up and be asking questions. Dr Harlow and Billy Damiani would both be in his sights.

People like Damiani always have problems, I reflected. In the end, they either go under or get a seat in the House of Lords. It could go either way.

'Something else: she said that Chloe had hinted that Brideswell was a place where things happened.'

'The episode again?'

'I reckon so, and if she was still talking about it when she'd left the estate agency business, that's interesting in itself. But she didn't seem frightened.'

'I wonder if she was there more than once?'

'She might have been. No evidence.'

We talked for a while after that, on a more personal level. About Kate, and about Annie Cooper, Kate's mother and my friend, who was getting through one of her madder periods.

Then I packed up all my papers, pushed them into my case, and took the whole lot back to Brideswell. I enjoyed the drive there, appreciating the soft autumn beauty of the woods and fields.

Muff was waiting for me, pacing the kitchen floor hungrily. She opened and closed her mouth several times in silent reproof. I wondered if she was missing Maid of Honour Row.

'The roof is nearly repaired,' I said, 'and we have windows, but you may be making a long stay in Brideswell, so get used to it.'

I lit the fire in the big front living room, standing for a moment to enjoy the blaze as the wood caught. Then I joined Muff in the kitchen, handing out her supper before I ate myself. Food was not important to me at the moment. Time to pause in thought was important.

I was a successful professional but I wasn't handling my life very well. By my behaviour when Chloe's body was discovered I had driven away a man I was fond of. I hesitated to use the words 'in love with', I wasn't sure if I was capable of that state any more, but Humphrey certainly aroused emotions I had thought dead.

I liked that arousal and disliked it at the same time. That was the root of it really, I was two-faced. In two minds. But it was idle to pretend my mood was entirely because of Humphrey.

I opened my case and took out all the reports and documents that I still needed to work on. I piled them on the table.

Chloe Devon had been in this house, my house. She had walked in the rooms, looked out of the window.

Billy Damiani had been here.

They had both been here. I didn't like it.

With a sigh which acknowledged my irrationality and weakness, I pulled the papers towards me and started work. I read, signed, initialled, and then began to put them away.

Among the last papers was a copy of further forensic work on Chloe Devon's remains. It had been argued that the one forensic laboratory should deal with all the different pieces.

Pieces, I said to myself. This is a human body you are talking about.

The report itself was matter of fact. An interim statement of progress for the benefit of the police team: work was continuing. Scientists expert on various different disciplines had been at work.

One group had discerned various particles of textiles, wool and cotton, which might be useful when a killer was eventually located. When further investigated these particles might even hint where he could be found.

It could happen, I knew.

There were flakes of skin particles which did not belong to Chloe, hence were probably the killer's.

At some point, Chloe's head and hair had been doused with disinfectant, perhaps to hide the smell of decay.

The head and trunk had been severed with rough force by a sharp blade. Probably the same as that used to separate the limbs already found. The style and cut was similar.

The final few sentences dealt with some bite marks on the neck which could now be compared with those on the hand discovered earlier. The scientist, who signed himself T. Trent and who was not known to me, said that in both cases he believed them to be marks made by teeth, but he was now reserving judgement on the animal origin of those teeth.

Teeth marks were a special area in which T. Trent was not expert. A forensic odontologist was being called upon.

I folded the papers away. I was picking up some strange vibrations here. Teeth belonging in an animal's mouth. But which animal had been in two different places? Chewing a severed hand in one place, and the girl's neck in another?

The forensic scientist was worried, I was worried. Chief Superintendent Barney, if he was not a fool, would also be worried. I wondered if I should make contact with him?

I had a hot bath, washed my hair (clean hair suddenly seemed important), then stood over the basin, cleaning my teeth hard. Clean teeth seemed important too.

We were carnivores, weren't we?

I was in the kitchen, making a hot drink while watching Muff, who seemed to be having bad dreams, when the doorbell rang. I let it ring again before going to the door. Even then I hesitated before opening it. Security was second nature to me, and I had the mobile telephone close by before I did.

Humphrey stood there. It was raining again and he was wet.

'I thought you'd gone for good,' I said.

85

NINE

He laughed. 'You know better than that.'

'It's late.' I held the door open wider, a gust of wet damp wind blew through. 'Come on in, and let me shut the door.'

He walked past me, and then turned back to look at me.

'I'm staying. That invitation, remember? I'm taking you up on it. I left the ring.'

'That was a message? I read it wrong. I thought it was goodbye.' I am too old for this, I thought.

'The sapphire is a family ring. I don't say goodbyes with it. In fact, I have never given it to anyone before.'

I looked at him cautiously. What about your wife, I thought.

He displayed the trick he had of reading my thoughts. 'No, not even to her.'

I took a deep breath. 'I thought you were angry.'

'I was. And I was right to be angry. One minute I was with you, important to you, I thought. Then the next minute, I'd gone. Down a black hole. Invisible.'

'I'm sorry.'

'You'd do it again tomorrow in the same cir-cumstances.'

I had to admit it. 'Probably. Yes, probably I would.'

'It's the first time I have seen you at work. It was a shock.'

I went over to the fire, which was dying down. I threw

86

a log on and waited for it to blaze. I was very conscious that I was wearing my old striped blue and white dressing-gown, and that the room was not tidy. These things matter; they shouldn't, but they have their own weight on behaviour and events. 'I have to share you with your work.'

'Share, yes, not to be totally obliterated. I wasn't there. You didn't see me or hear me.'

I moved away to the bookcase where the bottles and glasses still rested just as they had that first day when Crick and David had helped me. It was obviously going to be their permanent home. 'Let's have a drink.'

There was only one comfortable armchair among those I had bought and that fault would have to be remedied, but I had managed to choose some more cups and saucers from the Post Office, which seemed to stock everything. I pushed the hair back from my forehead and perched by the fire on the low, old-fashioned guard. It was a bit like sitting on a shooting stick but just bearable. 'I must get some more chairs. You take that one.' I poured him some whisky, but gave myself mineral water. I needed a clear mind and I knew I was tired enough for spirit to go straight to my head. I crouched by the fire, encouraging it to burn up with a poker.

'I did feel guilty afterwards.' The fire crackled and threw out some sparks. I extinguished them carefully on the oriental rug which had belonged to Mrs Armitage. 'My work doesn't usually cut across our relationship.' What I did not say was: And yet yours does, frequently, and no questions asked.

Perhaps it was allowed to men. I ceased to feel guilty.

'You look thoughtful.'

I studied my hands. 'Yes. I can't remake my life.'

'I don't want you to do anything like that. But I don't think this village, this house, is good for you.'

'Oh, that can't be so, you are imagining it.'

'Yes, it's taking you over.' He looked around. 'It'll

need a fortune spending on it, this house. And I've never liked Brideswell, it's a village with a strange feeling to it. And now the bits and pieces of that poor girl turning up here. You're fascinated by it, too interested.'

'It's my job.'

'I think it means more to you than that in this instance.'

I stared at him, wondering if it was true. 'It's difficult not to get involved.'

'I don't like the Cremornes either, and I'm not sure about this young one. He's not typical of them, Heaven knows.'

'You needn't be jealous.'

'Is that what I am? I don't think so . . . but you draw so far away sometimes.'

I moved closer and dropped my head on to his knees, leaning against him. 'I'm here now.'

He didn't say anything.

'I'm lonely sometimes,' I said.

The events of the night, happy as they were, solved nothing of our problems. I suppose the most you could say was that they took our minds off them.

I woke early and went down to the kitchen to make some coffee. The cat was asleep in her basket by the big stove. It seemed the natural place for a cat basket, warm and sheltered. The basket had almost walked there without outside help.

Instead of jumping straight from her basket as she usually did, Muff stayed there. Not curled up in a comfortable ball but slightly extended, her paws stretched out, her eyes half open. They had a shuttered look.

I knew at once that she was ill.

I sat at the big kitchen table, a legacy from the late owner, drinking the hot coffee while I thought about Muff.

When Humphrey came down the stairs and into the kitchen our eyes met in amused complicity. We might have our differences, we would always have them as far as I could see, but we liked each other.

I poured some coffee and pushed it across. 'I'm worried about the cat.'

He got up at once, bending over, and stroking her head. I liked him more at that moment of tenderness than I ever had. 'Better get the vet.'

'I believe Tim Abbey's van comes to the village today.' It was Friday, one of the days when the white van parked itself down by the church.

'Don't wait for that. Get him to call. You don't want to disturb the old lady.' He gave Muff a last stroke and came back to his coffee. 'I'll make the call if you like.'

'No, don't worry, finish your breakfast. There's toast and honey. That is, I haven't made the toast, but . . .'

'But I know how,' he finished for me.

'I'll make the call.' I got up. 'I'd better get dressed. I'll tell my secretary not to expect me this morning. She can deal with it.'

He looked at his watch. 'I ought to make some calls, if I may.'

'Yes, do,' I said with resignation, knowing full well that if things followed their usual pattern, then calls to Washington, Brussels, and Moscow would probably figure on my telephone bill. Humphrey seemed to manage local communication by telepathy while requiring constant expensive contact with overseas.

Muff raised her head and spewed out a pale yellow vomit. Some of it spattered on Humphrey. I hurried to tidy Muff and the floor. Humphrey tried to help but I pushed him aside.

'Go and have a bath. You smell terrible.'

'I think some of your scent has rubbed off on me.' He read something in my eyes. 'I suppose I gave it you for Christmas.'

I hesitated. 'My birthday actually.'

'I'll do better another time.'

89

'Try smelling it first and not going by the price on the bottle.' He closed the bathroom door.

I took a deep breath, then turned to get dressed. He had not given me the scent. Someone else had. I was turning out to be not a very nice person.

Tim Abbey arrived before I was ready, while I was still brushing my hair, so that I had to run down the stairs to meet him, arriving flushed and out of breath.

'Take it easy,' he said, in a friendly way.

'I'm glad you're here. Come and take a look.'

Muff had not moved, nor did she as he bent over her, but she looked at him with dull eyes.

He examined her, looking in her mouth, and feeling her abdomen, which seemed distended. 'I'll just take her temperature.' Muff had never suffered this indignity before, her eyes widened a fraction as he held up her tail and inserted the thermometer, as if this was not quite what she had expected. 'Yes, she has a bit of a fever.'

He sat back on his heels while he considered the matter. Then he looked up at me with merry, cheerful blue eyes, the bluest I had ever seen. 'Don't look so worried, I think we can cure her.' He searched in his bag producing a small phial into which he plunged a hypodermic. 'I'll just give an antibiotic and you can carry on with tablets. You can manage that, can you?'

Muff did not flinch as the injection went into the loose skin but she gave me the look of one who will not suffer this too often. Then her paw flashed out and raked his hand.

'Oh. I'm sorry.' I apologized for her.

'Don't worry, occupational hazard.' He dabbed some iodine on his left hand which was already badly marked by an old scar.

'Looks as if a puma got you there,' I said, looking at one sickle-shaped scar.

'A Peke. No one bites worse than a Peke. But don't worry, I heal well and so will your feline.'

'Yes,' I said, with relief. 'What is it she has?'

90

'Not sure. Some virus, I think.'

'She's had all her immunizations.'

'There's plenty to be picked up. And she's come to a new district.' He ran his hand over her. 'Come along, lady. Give us a purr.'

He must charm his patients into recovery, I thought. Or he would if they were human, but perhaps animals didn't respond to that sort of treatment. On the other hand, Muff looked brighter already.

Witchcraft, I thought, wondering what Ellen Bean made of him. She didn't like doctors, but how did she feel about veterinary surgeons? I could hear her saying: 'He's just built a fine new animal clinic, can't do that without a touch of magic.'

And she might well find him attractive, I thought as I watched him rise to his feet in one lithe muscular movement. I knew my friends Birdie and Winifred held that a healthy interest in sex was to be encouraged. ('I do, my dear, I do,' Winifred had said, casting down her eyes, 'one must practise what one preaches. The orgasm is a useful key to enlightenment.')

He stood up. 'Anyway, she looks comfortable enough there by the fire.'

'It seemed the right place for a cat basket.'

'Yes, it's where Mrs Armitage's cat slept. Old Tiger, nice cat.'

'I didn't know she had a cat.'

'Yes.' He sounded sad, as if he had minded. 'I had to put him down just before she died.'

'He was ill?'

'Oh, yes, or I wouldn't have done it.'

'They were sick together?'

'More or less the same symptoms, vomiting and so on,' he said reluctantly. 'Not from the same cause, of course. Probably just old age with Tiger. His kidneys were packing up. He'd been around a long time. Still, I was sorry to see him go.'

He handed me a bottle of tablets. 'Two a day. And if you're worried, call me.' He packed away his bag.

He was on the way out when the telephone rang. I hesitated. 'Do answer it,' he said. 'I'll see myself out.'

'No, wait. I won't be a minute. Hello?'

A strange voice answered me. It sounded drunk. 'Thomas Dryden here.'

'Oh, Mr Dryden,' I said in surprise. 'What is it?'

'Like to see you. Speak to you.'

'Really? What about?' I asked cautiously. I wanted him to go on talking: I thought I recognized his voice, he could have been the caller who tried to put me off moving to the village.

'Tell you when I see you. Tonight. I'll come to the house.' He put the telephone down with a bang.

Tim Abbey looked at me and raised an eyebrow. 'Our village drunk. Don't let him be a nuisance.'

'I won't.'

'He's not a bad sort,' said Abbey, thoughtfully.

I saw him to the door, where he paused. 'Don't worry. I think your creature is going to be fine. I can't be sure, but I think she may just have caught something and eaten it, and it doesn't agree with her.'

I looked back and met Muff's mournful gaze. 'Just tummy ache?'

I went to the stairs and called up. 'You can come down now.'

Humphrey descended the stairs. 'Can I drive you in to Windsor?'

'No, I'll stay with Muff today. See how she is.'

'You really love her.'

'I don't know about love. She needs looking after.'

'And you don't think you need a child.'

I didn't react, didn't even change the expression on my face. It is so easy to hit someone even without meaning to when you know them very well; I didn't want him to know he had hurt.

But I had a response. Of a kind.

'About the scent. You didn't give it to me. Someone else did.'

'I thought I couldn't have done. I do smell what I give as a present.'

'It didn't mean anything. And anyway, he's dead.'

'Ah. Because of you?'

'Yes, because of me, but not the way it sounds.'

I tidied the house, I was getting to be quite a housewife. Then I went to the baker's shop for a loaf and a bottle of milk.

Inside I met Ellen Bean, who was buying a lardie cake, hot and steaming. Also, as I had discovered, exceedingly indigestible.

'I see you had the vet?'

'Yes, Muff wasn't well.'

'You'd have done better to call me in.'

'He was good with Muff.'

'Good with all animals.' Ellen gave a hoot of laughter. 'Might call him in myself next time I've got gut-ache.'

'He certainly is remarkably handsome,' I said in a neutral voice. I paid for my loaf and went to the door.

'He's got a lovely young girlfriend living with him,' said Ellen. 'You've met her, and I expect you'll see her in the van. She does some of the driving. Lu, she's called.'

'I spoke to her.' Now I had seen Tim Abbey I saw that they matched.

'Don't worry about your cat,' said Ellen. 'I saw her eating a bloody great rat . . . that's what she's got inside her. It'll pass through. I'll say the right words when I get home. Say them now if you like.'

'No, leave it,' I said hastily. 'At home will do.'

'Privacy is better, you wouldn't expect me to be embarrassed with all my experience, but you do get some funny looks sometimes . . . She's quite a hunter, your cat, I saw her at it. The ratling didn't have a chance.'

93

It was a relief to know that it was only indigestion, but it did summon up a picture of my cat Muff, wild in the grass. 'Sounds dangerous,' I said. 'I wish she wouldn't.'

'I'll send my cat to keep an eye on her.'

'How will I know him, what's he like?'

'A big black bugger,' said Ellen with gusto.

'What's he called?'

'His village name is Blackie, but his devil name is Belial,' she said with evident satisfaction.

It was very hard to know if she was laughing at me or not.

'Watch your step,' she called after me.

As I walked down the village street I observed that the press was there as well as the police. A big TV van had settled into position by the Red Dragon. So far no one had noticed me, but I was reasonably well known by now for someone in the media band to recognize me and I had no desire to be interviewed, quoted, misquoted, or photographed. I put my head down and moved towards my house. The Red Dragon would be out of bounds for me until the caravan moved on.

Muff was still in her basket, she looked up at me. I stroked her head to be rewarded with a faint purr. She was coming back to life.

I was surprised by a ring at the front door. I considered ignoring it, but even as I stood there in thought, the bell rang again.

To my surprise it was Chief Superintendent Barney. 'All right if I come in, ma'am?' He was being carefully formal.

I held the door wide. 'Yes, of course. Anything I can do?'

'Probably is, ma'am. Can we talk about it inside?' He sounded gloomy. I had been told that he took things heavily and was not a man to laugh off a setback in an investigation. I didn't dislike him for that. Murder is a serious business. 'I'm afraid I was seen coming in.' He looked over his shoulder. 'Got me in the frame.'

'Doesn't matter.' I was resigned to publicity without welcoming it. I used it when I had to – in some cases you need help from the media – but otherwise I preferred anonymity. I drew up a chair by the window seat. I could keep an eye on the road from there and even see the encampment outside the Red Dragon.

I was uncomfortably aware that I was wearing jeans and a sweater and that my hair was untidy, whereas Clive Barney, although looking tired and worried, was dressed with neatness and precision. His shoes shone.

'I thought it would be best if we talked the investigation over together. I know you get the formal reports but I don't want you to have the feeling that I am keeping you out of it when you are on the spot.' He paused. 'I know you're taking an interest.'

I nodded without saying anything. He knew about Rewley, then? Well, he would. No secrets in our business. There were matters we kept quiet about, of course, but very few of importance that were not known.

'We aren't getting anywhere. But I expect you knew that?' He paused, waiting to see if I said anything and when I didn't went on: 'We've run through everything and come out the other end with nothing.'

'Everything?'

'What I call everything. We had two prime men to focus on.'

I nodded again.

'As far as Dr Harlow is concerned . . . He looked likely but there's nothing to lay our hands on. No evidence he knew her, nothing from forensics on his clothes or his house that connects him. And we've been thorough about that.'

I knew the team would have been. 'The car?'

'Nothing there. We're completely stalled.'

I stood up. 'Like some coffee? Or something stronger.'

'Coffee, decaff if you've got it.'

That fitted in too. He was reported to be an insomniac worrier, a perfectionist who got results but paid for it.

From the kitchen I called: 'What about the knife cuts, anything there?'

He came and stood at the kitchen door. 'A competent powerful chopping job, but no signs of skilled surgical knowledge. Not professional at all. But if it was the doctor you would expect him to take trouble to cover up.' He accepted a cup of coffee, it was the full job, loaded with caffeine, but I didn't tell him, it might cheer him up. 'And if he did cut her up, he didn't do it in his own backyard. No signs of blood in the bathroom or kitchen. Some in the surgery washplace, but that's understandable, being what it is.'

'Worth thinking about, though.'

'Oh, I have, don't you worry, we're running checks on the blood groups, but I doubt if he could get away with much in the surgery with a nurse and receptionist like he has. Eagle eyed and miss nothing, both of them.' He grinned, making his face suddenly look younger and more friendly. 'They were able to tell me without any trouble that the doctor has a girl in Reading, a colleague he sleeps with twice a month in Oxford, and an ex-wife in Salisbury, and seems to be on good terms with all of them. And there are thought to be others.'

'What about the teeth marks on parts of the body? Anything new?'

'Still waiting for the special report. These things take time.' He paused. 'Nasty, though.'

'Unpleasant,' I said. 'Have you checked on animals in the village?'

He groaned. 'This is the country: there are rats, dogs, ferrets, and God knows what else.'

We both sat in silence for a moment, neither of us wanting to say another word about the tooth marks.

'Coffee all right?' I asked.

'Fine, ma'am, you make a good cup. Could I have some more sugar? I know I shouldn't but I can't seem to manage without since I gave up smoking.' His nose twitched reminiscently as if he could scent smoke and missed it. He was relaxing the formality. 'I know you know Damiani,' he said suddenly.

'No secret there.'

It was time to clear the air. 'He is *not* a friend,' I said firmly. 'And I regard him as a prime suspect.'

'He knew the girl,' said Barney. 'Her took her to the village, he gave her dinner, he was there. He was the last person we know she was with. Yes, I suspect him. Still do, but I can't get anything positive on him.'

There was no doubt that both of us would have liked to get something on Billy Damiani.

'With both suspects looking clean there's only one way forward at the moment: we'll question all the village men, one by one, and take body samples.'

I nodded. It was a dogged, hateful piece of drudgery, but it would have to be done.

'Have you come across Thomas Dryden?'

Barney nodded. 'The name has come up.'

'He seems to be in a strange state.' Of course, not all strange states led to murder. 'He might be worth looking at.'

'He's on the list,' said Barney. He had brightened up considerably as he drank the coffee. He might have an insomniac night, his hands might be jumpy, but he was a happier man.

'One other thing; some weeks ago. I had a telephone call trying to put me off moving here,' I said. 'A man's voice; I didn't recognize it.' I shrugged. 'Might be mean nothing, might be something. It could have been him.'

'Dryden?'

'Yes.'

He considered in the dour, thoughtful way in which I suspect he considered all new, possibly exciting information. 'If anything occurs to you, let me know.' He finished his coffee and put down his cup, then stood up, preparing to go.

'Just one more thing. You didn't know the village well before you came to the house?'

I shook my head. 'No, I came once or twice with a friend.'

'Would that be the Lady Mary Dalmeny Erskine?'

'Yes, it was with Mary. This house belonged to her aunt.'

'Oh yes, Mrs Armitage. You didn't know her?'

'No, she died before Mary brought me to the village.'

He was nearly at the door and then he stopped. 'You didn't know the dead girl yourself?'

'No, I never met her.'

I realized then that he was getting round to his real reason for coming.

'Had you even heard of her?'

'No, what is this?'

He paused ominously before replying. 'A piece of paper with your name and Windsor address was in the pocket of the dress she wore when she was killed.'

I stared at him.

'She knew you, even if you didn't know her.'

I did not try to hide my anger. 'That was devious of you. Why didn't you ask straight away if I knew Chloe Devon?'

Barney took his time to answer. 'You have no idea how terrifying you are, ma'am. I couldn't do it.'

I was left not knowing if he spoke seriously or not.

After Clive Barney had gone, I found myself liking the man much more than I had expected. There was a kind of raw honesty about him that I had to respect.

He had thrown a small bombshell at me with the news that Chloe Devon had had my name and address. It made me jumpy, silly but true. It seemed bad news. I was

98

thinking about this as I went to look at Muff. She was warm and comfortable in the kitchen, but I needed more heat in the big front room where I intended to work. The ashes from yesterday were still warm and twigs and logs thrown on would soon light, but the basket of logs was nearly empty.

I was still using the wood and coal that Mrs Armitage had left behind, the logs were piled up outside in the garden. The rain had stopped so I took the log basket on my arm, filling it from the covered heap by the back door.

To the right was the flight of stone stairs to the outside store room where, according to my friend Lady Mary, had slept the unhappy menservants of the Victorian household. The steps themselves were damp and moss covered, mute testimony to their present day lack of use. Good job too, I thought, wondering how many of the original sleepers had died of pneumonia.

I had never given it a look, scarcely thought about it, but now curiosity drove me down the steps to push at the door. It opened with a scratching, screeching sound of hard old wood on stone, but it opened. There was not much to see inside, some light came through a slit-like window high in the wall. A flagged door, whitewashed stone walls, and a smell of damp and earth.

Nothing here, a few stains that I might have imagined to be blood if I was feeling imaginative, an old dustbin, which was empty, and a rusty-looking fire extinguisher.

I closed the door, it had no key in the lock, then mounted the steps. I was nearly at the top when my foot slipped on a scattering of greasy leaves, and I fell backwards, hitting my head on the stone walls as I went.

Watch your step, Ellen Bean had said, damn her.

TEN

It was Nora Garden, calling to ask after Muff, who found me, staggering up the steps with blood streaming down my face. She took me inside and called the doctor. 'And pleased to come,' she reported. 'Once the police took their teeth out of him, all he wanted was a patient. A bloody patient, and you are bloody, dear, and that's a nasty black eye coming up, just did the trick.'

He was driving round to see me, no doubt appreciating the irony of helping a police officer.

'I don't think I need a doctor.'

'I thought you did,' said Nora. 'I was the one who found you. You probably have a slight concussion.'

She was prowling around my living room, moving everything she touched. 'You really must make it more comfortable in here. You haven't got enough furniture.'

'I'm getting more,' I muttered. Speech was difficult, my mouth felt sore. Had I broken a tooth? I ran my tongue over them cautiously. No, all there and no jagged edges. 'It takes time, that's all.' I flexed my foot cautiously. 'I think I've sprained my ankle.'

'You ought to be lying down.' She looked around the room. 'But there's nowhere to lay you.'

She had propped me up in the one big armchair, and was herself leaning against the bookcase. Perhaps she had a point, the room was bare. But I thought that already it had its own comfort, it was a happy room, full of light and warmth. The fire was blazing nicely; Nora must have

100

piled on the logs. At least I had managed to get them up out of the store room. She must have carried them inside though.

I raised my head from the cushion. 'Don't use all the wood or I shall have to get some more in.'

'Is that what you were doing? Thought you were.'

'In part.' I shifted uncomfortably in the chair. 'Just having a look round.'

'It's a terrible place. You could hide a body in it.'

'What a truly awful thing to say.'

Nora looked surprised. 'Sorry, spoke without thinking. It's that poor girl . . . Of course, I'm not suggesting she was hidden in . . .'

A wave of irritation swept over me. 'I wish you hadn't called in the doctor.'

Nora looked down at me with a gentle smile. In her last TV series she had played a nurse and I could see she was still living the part. 'I did consider Ellen Bean.'

'Heaven forbid.' Perhaps it wasn't such a bad idea to see Dr Harlow; I could observe him at close quarters. Could a doctor be a killer? Well, I knew he could be. A grisly catalogue went through my mind: Dr Palmer, the poisoner; Crippen, if you could count him as a doctor, his medical qualifications were not profound; Dr Buck Ruxton, and there were others.

'Ellen's quite a healer in her way. She did a good job on my toe.'

I nursed my foot. Ellen was probably responsible for what had happened to me: 'Watch your step,' she had said.

Nora was enjoying all this. I remembered now that the nurse in that TV series had also been a sleuth. She was called a sleuth, it was that sort of TV series, Nurse Foggerty. Much loved, I believe. 'Ah, here he is.'

Dr Harlow came in then, with a sort of swagger. He was a tall, dark-haired man, with the broad shoulders that probably demanded a swagger. Well, nothing wrong

101

in that perhaps, not all swaggerers were beasts, although I had an instinctive dislike of them, having met too many in my time.

He had kind brown eyes and a gentle voice, though. Equally, I knew from my own experience that kind eyes and gentle voices might not count for much.

Nora retreated. 'Leave you two together. Got to feed the cat. Back with some coffee.'

I was right, she was enjoying it.

He had large and not particularly gentle hands. I winced as he fingered my forehead and prodded my ankle.

'Nothing broken, and if you didn't lose consciousness . . .'

'Not for a moment.' I wasn't too sure about that, although I had no intention of saying so. I did not remember the arrival of Nora. Suddenly, she was there.

'Then no concussion, but you'll have a nasty bruise and a bad headache . . . I can give you some painkillers. I'll strap the ankle.'

I could hear Nora banging away at china in the kitchen, cupboard doors shutting, her voice talking to Muff and Muff not answering back.

'I think that ought to help.' He moved back from my foot.

'Feels better already.'

'You'll be able to walk if you don't put too much weight on it. Use a stick if you've got one. And rest it. Rest yourself too, you've been lucky, you could have broken your neck.'

'I know I could.'

He sat down and looked at me, his face suddenly tired. 'I will have some coffee if Nora's really making some.'

'I think she is. I can smell it.' I would need to get some more coffee. I seemed to be using a lot today.

'This isn't the best of times for you to get to know the village. But perhaps you don't mind?'

102

'Because of what I am?' I shook my head. 'It's never good.'

'No point in telling you that I didn't kill the girl?'

'Not my case.'

'And you're not interested?'

'Well . . .' I didn't finish the sentence. He knew that I must be interested, just as he would be if a sudden and unusual wave of illness spread through the village. 'Do you know Thomas Dryden?'

'Only as a villager. He isn't on my list. I don't have many patients from Brideswell, most of them go to Franklin in Tuppett's Halt.' This was the next village.

'I'm interested in him.'

'He's had bad luck, that man,' said Dr Harlow with the sympathy of one who felt he was having bad luck himself. 'Terrible tragedy with his wife . . . But she never got over the death of her brother and his wife and child. I think she blamed herself. Not her fault of course.'

Nora came back with a tray of coffee. 'I had a job to find enough cups . . . you don't seem to have more than one of anything.' She handed out a mug for me, a decent-looking cup for Dr Harlow, and the next best for herself. None of my Brideswell china was elegant but it was clean and unchipped.

Not much more was said. Dr Harlow finished his coffee quickly, collected his bag and coat, and departed.

When he'd gone, she tucked a blanket round me, Nurse Foggerty doing her stuff, and prepared to depart. 'Now you have a nice rest. I'll be back later on to see how you are.'

It was my intention to get up the moment the front door closed behind her, but to my surprise, my eyelids felt heavy, I was warm and comfortable, my headache was receding.

Muff crept up and settled on my lap. We both slept.

*

103

I was roused by the sound of voices and laughter. I recognized Kate's strong, deep tones. She was there and so was Rewley. The laughter came from Nora Garden.

'How did you get in?'

'I have a key,' said Nora. 'Always had one. Bea Armitage gave it me. I used come in and feed her cat if she was away. And you haven't changed the lock.'

'I might think of it,' I said, sitting up. Muff had gone and the fire was out.

'I'll give you the key back.'

Kate kissed my cheek. 'We came to see you as soon as we heard about your accident. George, do something about the fire.'

'Why have you come?'

'I heard you'd had an accident. I was worried. You weren't attacked, were you?'

'I fell.'

She shook her head. 'Not like you. How do you feel?'

'Fine, I'm better. I am officially better.'

'You could use some make-up on that eye.'

I got up and hobbled to the door. 'I'll put some on.'

I had already met Rewley's eyes and guessed from the look he gave me that his motive for calling had not been solely to mete out sympathy: he had something to tell me.

And since he could have spoken to me on the telephone, then he must also wish to consult or discuss.

When I came down the stairs, neat and tidy again, he was waiting for me. 'I've been sent out to make a tray of tea. Come and talk . . . It's Damiani.'

'Leave it to me. Tell me what you have on Damiani.'

Rewley filled the kettle and plugged it in before speaking. 'It's what he was up to the night Chloe Devon disappeared.'

'That was almost certainly when she was killed.'

'Yes, hard to be sure from the state of the body, but yes, the guess is she was killed almost at once. Dissected later.'

I flinched at the word. Rewley could be clinically cold sometimes. 'Get on with it, please.'

'Damiani said he went back to London where he called on his sister. She confirmed that . . . But I've discovered that she herself was out at a private party and did not return home until the small hours.'

'Barney must have checked.'

'Oh, he did. It's in the records. But Bridget Damiani's hostess lied. Said she left early. Early enough to have been there when her brother said she was.'

I didn't ask him how he knew, being fully aware that Rewley had his own methods and contacts, but I did want to know why the hostess had lied. I think I could almost have guessed the answer.

'She had an affair with Damiani . . . she's in love with him.'

'Why didn't he go to her and cut out the sister?'

Rewley smiled. 'She has a husband,' he said.

'Silly question.'

'He did turn up, but several hours later than he said. The taxi driver who brought the sister back saw him arrive.'

The kettle was boiling so I infused the tea. I washed all the used cups and found two more. If I was to take my residence here seriously then Nora was right: I must buy still more china and furniture. People were always dropping in.

But did I really mean to stay? Or were my hesitations a reflection of an inner intention not to stay? The house in Brideswell was my declaration of independence. Once made, did I secretly intend to go back to Maid of Honour Row?

I dragged my mind back to Billy Damiani, liar and deceiver. But we all lie when pushed and I was playing a fair hand of deception myself. 'So what was he doing all that time?'

'He could have been killing Chloe Devon.'

105

'Keep this to yourself for the moment while I think about it.'

We carried the tea things in between us. I was limping, my ankle felt sore, my black eye was developing with every moment, but I felt better.

I was pouring out the tea while Kate told me exactly how I would redecorate and furnish my house if I listened to her, when I heard the sound of a car stopping outside.

Rewley went to the window, he watched, then turned with a raised eyebrow. 'Damiani, and Lady Mary.'

They came in together, bringing a gust of cold air with them. 'I had to come,' said Mary. 'I heard you'd been attacked. I made Billy bring me.'

'Glad to do it,' he said, being the gallant gentleman. 'How are you?'

'I was not attacked, I fell, entirely my own fault. How did you know?'

'David and Crick telephoned.'

'I told them,' said Nora quickly. 'They will be dropping in too, I expect.'

'And Ellen Bean?'

'Of course, not her husband, though, he has a church meeting in Reading. Otherwise, of course, he'd be here with the vicar.'

'I hope you're joking.'

'Oh, we take visiting the sick seriously in Brideswell.' Once more it was hard to be sure if she was laughing at me or not.

But true enough, in a few moments the bell rang again and Crick and David were in the room.

There were no clean tea cups left, but some sherry was produced. I think Nora must have brought a bottle with her. She had certainly been responsible for the seed cake and vanilla sponge that appeared for tea.

'I expected to see Thomas Dryden today,' I said as I handed David his sherry. 'But not all of you.'

'Better off with us,' he said. 'How's Muff?'

106

'On my bed asleep, as far as I know.'

Billy Damiani took up a place by the fire and put down his sherry; he reached for Mary's hand. To my surprise, she blushed.

'Mary and I had another reason in coming. I expect you can guess: Lady Mary has done me the honour of agreeing to be my wife.'

I stared at Mary. The colour retreated from her face leaving just a faint circle of red around her eyes.

'Show them, Mary.'

She held out her left hand; the steely blue gleam of a really large diamond shone there. Just like Billy Damiani to have a huge diamond ready for use.

'Good Lord, is it real?' said David, and then apologized. 'Of course it is.' He went over and kissed her cheek. 'My very best wishes. I always fancied you myself.'

Money does give power, I thought. David has none, Lady Mary very little, her soldier boy even less: Billy Damiani was rich. He was pulling the strings.

Money was important here in this case. Intuitively, I knew this to be the case.

Money was king.

None of them stayed long but Nora departed first and then Mary and Damiani. Crick and David went soon after.

'Has good memories, this house has,' said David, giving me a parting kiss on the cheek. 'Want you to be happy in it. Part of the village.'

'As you are. Thank you, David.'

'If I am, not sure I always feel it,' he said. 'Come on, Crick.'

I closed the door. I could just see Ellen Bean poking her nose round the gate as if she was considering what to do. She might call, she might not, it didn't matter, the air waves or her black cat would keep her informed of what went on.

I stood there waiting to see if she rang the bell and remembering Lady Mary. As she departed, I had put my arm round her.

'Are you all right? Is it all right?'

'Shut up,' she said, with a wry smile.

Not good, I thought, not good at all.

Only Kate and Rewley remained. Kate curled herself on the window seat and stared out.

Rewley said: 'There's something to tell you. I was watching when Damiani and Mary arrived. I saw his face, I could read what he said. He said to her: "Keep your mouth shut and follow what I say. Do that and we shall be all right." '

I considered. 'Not very loving.'

'No, not a very loving look on his face. And as he rang the bell, he said: "I wish I had never come to this damned house." '

'Rewley,' I said. 'Go and look in the outside cellar. Tell me what you think of some stains on the floor and wall. See if you think it's blood.'

'Is it likely to be?'

'I don't know. Just take a look . . . Would you mind?'

He knew an order when he heard one.

He said quickly, 'I'll go down and see what I make of it.'

Kate and I sat in a temporary peace. Muff reappeared. She sidled up beside me and I stroked her head. Then Rewley returned. Quiet as always, he waited until he could see me alone. There was no doubt in my mind about his abilities, he would go straight to the top, he knew how to do things.

'I had an inspection. A couple of very battered rusty fire extinguishers, looking a health hazard. And yes, there are stains, and I would say they were blood.'

I waited for him to say something more. 'Have to get it checked,' he said. 'May be something, may be nothing.'

108

Then I said: 'Chloe Devon had a piece of paper with my name and address on it in her pocket,' I said. I felt aggrieved.

He was well informed as ever. 'I had heard.'

'Really?'

'The word got around.'

'I'll tell Clive Barney about the cellar,' I said. 'Damn, damn and damn.'

Perhaps Humphrey was right: I should never have moved into this house. Of all my friends, he was the one who had not yet rushed to see me.

ELEVEN

I telephoned Clive Barney myself to tell him about the possible blood stains. Better to be straight with it, I thought.

He took it calmly. 'Could be anything, animal blood most likely. But worth a look.'

Then I telephoned Humphrey. No answer. And again. Still no answer.

I was alone in the house now, except for Muff.

I don't mind being alone as a rule, in fact, in many ways I prefer it, but tonight I would have liked Humphrey to be there, making up the fire so that it blazed, then eating dinner with me.

He came eventually, tired and not willing to talk much. He was sympathetic about my accident without seeming much concerned. It dawned on me that I had already dwindled into a wife.

A dangerous position to be in, as everyone knows.

Next day was a working day. I limped but was otherwise fit. Muff also seemed to have recovered, although she was not as hungry as usual.

I was made aware that a police team had been in my cellar, scratching around. When I got back home that evening I saw the signs. They had sealed the door and barred off the stairs. Eventually I got a message that

110

nothing had been removed but samples had been scraped and photographs taken.

Interesting and significant, I thought.

That day, before leaving for the country I had called at Maid of Honour Row, where no great progress had been made that I could see; rather the reverse, the poor little house looked worse. The house was in a mess, with builders' ladders and equipment all over it. I stood in the middle of my sitting room there while I wondered if I would ever move back. Then I packed a box of china to take back to Brideswell.

I had a passenger too. My friends, the Windsor white witches, Winifred Eagle and Birdie Peacock, with whom my dog Benjy usually lived (he preferred it), had gone off for a Conference on Natural Healing in Bath, and Benjy was in my charge.

He liked a car ride so he travelled hopefully. Round his neck was a label inscribed by Winifred saying: *I have not had my walk today, please give me one.* I looked anxiously out of the window, a thick mist hung over the valley in which Brideswell lay, and these narrow lanes took some navigating. It would be very easy to miss the Brideswell turn. But there it was, and I took it gratefully. The mist seemed heavier here, the trees were completely shrouded.

It was with some relief I drew up outside my house. There it was, sitting firmly in the village street as it had done for two hundred years. I unpacked the car, allowed Muff and Benjy (not natural friends) to get to know each other again. Then I took Benjy for the walk Miss Eagle had requested.

I walked down the street, already darkening. It looked like rain again now as the mist grew even thicker and wetter. Benjy ran ahead, sniffing joyfully. This was good, he was saying, this was what a dog liked. The damp air had thickened into a fog which hung over the roofs,

111

wreathing spirals of cloud over the trees, obscuring the vista of the church at the end of the road.

Benjy shot ahead of me and trotted into the church-yard, where he began to bark, high excited yelps.

I stood at the gate calling him, then I saw someone staggering towards me down the path. As I looked, the figure slid to the ground.

I bent over the form, a man, lying face down on the earth. The back of the head had been hit, I could see the bone and blood. Gently I turned him over.

The face, too, was covered with blood, blood had poured down over the front of his chest, soaking his sweater. Beneath the blood I could make out that the face itself had been gouged. Sliced.

The hands had been cut as well, in exactly the same way.

In spite of the damage, I knew I was looking at Thomas Dryden. He had not been rendered unrecognizable. If that had been the intention of the killer, then it had failed.

I sat back on my heels.

A noise, a thick uttering. Behind the bloody mask, he was speaking.

'One of them was murdered.'

TWELVE

Ellen Bean was standing on the pavement outside the church. 'Heard the dog,' she said.

'Anyone would.' I had Benjy tethered close to me, but he was wailing now like a lost soul, his excited barks having given way before the conviction that something alarming was afoot.

She patted his head, then walked past me towards the churchyard.

'Don't go on,' I said sharply.

Ellen ignored the order, she marched in and was lost to sight in the mist. For the first time I noticed she was wearing a thick tweed cloak and carrying a stick as if prepared for trouble.

She was soon back. 'So they got the poor devil.'

'They?'

'He, she, or it,' said Ellen. 'They. Figure of speech.' She gave me a sharp stare. 'You look terrible. I'll go down to the Incident Room and tell Clive Barney.' She had it all off pat, even to Barney's name. She'd probably had several interesting talks with him. Offered to read his future or identify the killer.

I gathered myself together; I hooked Benjy on to a spur on the iron gate so that he could not follow me. 'Tell him to call an ambulance urgently. It's just possible . . .'

She gave me a startled look and, to her justice, scuttled off at once. I heard her say: 'Oh, my dear Lord.'

I took a deep breath; I was frightened, an emotion I

113

do not usually allow myself, but there was evidence of such terrible brutality in what I had just seen. But I knew what I had to do and I went back into the churchyard to kneel by Thomas Dryden. I took his hand to feel for the pulse. The flesh was still warm and I thought I could feel a very faint throb beneath my fingers.

A little blood was bubbling from his lips which I wiped away. I whispered in his ear.

'Help is coming,' I said. 'Hang on. Just hang on.'

Was he trying to speak again? To say something more? I wanted to spare him the agony of trying.

'I heard,' I said. 'I heard: one of them was murdered.' I wanted to spare the agony of speech but I had to know more. 'Who? Who was murdered?'

From between his lips came another bubble of blood. A breath seemed to move between his lips. I put my head close so that I could hear.

'Fire,' he seemed to be saying. 'Fire.'

'Fire?' I wondered what he meant, or even if I was hearing correctly. 'Who did this to you? Can you say?'

But there was nothing more. Only those tears of blood around his eyes and the seepage from his mouth. His lips relaxed, perhaps he was gone. But no, still that ghost of a pulse.

Ghosts, I thought, sitting back on my heels, if there wasn't a ghost in Brideswell already, then there would be after this act of slaughter. A bloody weeping ghost.

Ellen came running back, I heard Benjy give a small bark as she sped past. Behind her came the heavier tread of Clive Barney.

I hadn't expected him.

Barney acknowledged me with a slight nod, then he bent down over Dryden. 'What's this then?'

'As you see,' I said. 'I found him. I don't know how he got here or how this happened. But he didn't do it to himself.'

Barney grunted a no. He shook his head. 'Ambulance

114

is on the way.' He stood up and took me aside. He acted from a delicacy I had not expected.

'He may still be able to hear, wouldn't want that. Is he still alive?'

'Just. Barely.'

'They're the worst injuries I've ever seen, and I've seen some. They look deliberate too. No accident.' He added: 'Don't think he'll make it.'

'Can't be sure.'

'Has he said anything?'

I hesitated. 'I can only tell you what I think I heard.' I told him.

Barney repeated my words back to me. ' "One of them was murdered." And then "Fire" . . . was it really fire?'

'I don't know. Sounded like it. Might have been almost anything: iron, ire, wire.'

'And he couldn't say how he was attacked?'

I shook my head.

'Pity.' He took a pace away from me and then swung round. 'It has to be connected with the other business.'

He made it a question, he wanted my opinion.

'I think so.'

'But what he said: "One of them was murdered" . . . What the hell does that mean?'

No answer there. I had none to give. 'We might find out.'

'We might. We ought to but will we?' He added shortly: 'Not much joy on the Chloe Devon killing. We're sweeping the village, all the males, but no go.'

He turned back to kneel by Dryden's body. 'I think he's gone.'

I could see the lights of the ambulance approaching, hear Benjy's bark. 'Do you believe in evil?'

He answered promptly. 'Yes, sure. Seen plenty of it.'

'There's evil in this village.'

Clive Barney hesitated before he answered this time. 'That's not like you, ma'am.' I could see he did not know

115

how to handle it. Not like the tough-minded careerist Charmian Daniels whom we all know and love to hate, he meant. 'I don't see it that way,' he went on. 'When we get the killer, if we ever do, then we will find he had a good practical motive for the whole lot.'

Ellen and the two ambulance men came hurrying up the path. One of them had a large torch that doubled as a lamp.

'Dear God,' said one of them when he saw Dryden.

If I believed in a God, I thought, other than a sort of demonaic figure that might suit Ellen Bean's demiworld, I would lay this day and its exhaustions at his feet and say: 'You deal with this.' As it was, I said: 'I'll go in the ambulance with him.'

'I'll take you in the car,' said Barney, quickly. 'Follow behind.'

'I'm going in the ambulance.' If anything was to come through those bloody lips, then I wanted to hear.

'I really shouldn't, miss,' said the paramedic with the lamp. He was dealing expertly with Dryden. 'No room.'

'I'm not miss,' I said bleakly. 'I'm a senior police officer, and I am coming.' I saw Ellen on the path, her eyes bright and intent. 'Take the dog,' I said. She looked surprised but nodded, and unhooked Benjy from the gate.

But when I was in the ambulance, crouched to one side, and I saw how they had an oxygen mask on that torn-up face, and drips attached to his arm, saw how he was gagged and fettered, I realized that Thomas Dryden would not, could not utter.

Do doctors realize, I asked myself as I leaned against the side of the ambulance, how like the victims of medieval torture their bound-up, tied-up, muzzled patients look?

My energy drained away, I slumped on the floor, spent. No notice was taken of me as the ambulance sped through the mist, I was just extra luggage.

Then Dryden moved. Perhaps the oxygen was sparking

116

something inside him. He dragged at his mask and knocked at the oxygen tank at his side, almost seemed to be pushing away.

He wants to die, I thought, he's had enough. He's signalling he wants out and we won't let him go.

I took his hand. 'I should like to have known you,' I said. 'I shall remember you.'

A team of nurses and doctors was waiting for the ambulance. I stood aside, watching. I was aware of but took no notice of, the arrival of Clive Barney in the police car. He positioned himself just behind me; he had one or two acolytes with him.

There was a flurry of activity inside the ambulance, and then suddenly, it was all over. The doctors emerged to stand talking and the nurses walked away. As one of the doctors turned round, a tall, fair young woman with strong bones, I realized I knew her.

'Rosie.'

She looked at me with surprised recognition. 'Hello.'

I had met Rosie Meadows when she was dealing with a murder at the Prince Consort Hospital in Merrywick near Windsor. She had been a young houseman, assisting one of the surgeons at a time when I had been investigating a murder in the hospital car park.

'I'm senior casualty officer,' she said.

'Rosie, what's going on?' Or not going on, the ambulance was closing the doors and moving away with Dryden still inside. I suppose I knew what it meant deep down inside me, but I wanted someone to put it into speech, and doctors sometimes prefer silence.

'Dead on arrival,' said Rosie. She shook her head. 'We don't admit them then . . . they go elsewhere.'

I could pinpoint the moment of Dryden's death: the second after he had hit the oxygen bottle. Perhaps he had already been dead and it had been nothing more than a spasm of the dying organism. But it had looked deliberate, aimed. I believed with his last energies he had aimed at the oxygen flask. Perhaps it reminded him of something.

'I know the place you mean.' At that moment I did not wish to name the mortuary. I looked for the Chief Inspector, but he had already withdrawn to his car where he was talking on the telephone. I knew what he was doing: making arrangements for the police surgeon and the police pathologist to view Dryden's body.

'Is he one of yours?' she asked. 'I mean the dead man?'

'In a way,' I said. 'I found him.'

'Yes.' She looked at me speculatively. 'Would you like to tidy up? There's quite a bit of blood on your face. You weren't hurt yourself?'

I looked down on my hands. Dried blood there too. 'No, nothing like that. Yes, I'd like to wash.'

'You look as though you could do with a cup of coffee,' Rosie said as she led the way. 'And I know I could. Been on duty all day.'

In the wash room she handed me a clean towel. I studied my face which was streaked with dark blood. I even had some dark thick clumps of something in my hair. I did the best I could with soap and hot water.

'I could let you have some lipstick and powder,' said Rosie.

'Don't bother. I'll take the coffee, though.'

I didn't have to wonder about Clive Barney, he had gone off to get on with all the questions. He might never get the answers but he would be asking the questions.

As she poured the coffee, Rosie said thoughtfully: 'He was certainly done over, never seen anything quite like his injuries, not even in a car-crash death.'

'What killed him? Could you tell?'

'I'm not sure, not easy to make a good examination in the ambulance, but someone gave him a mighty bash on the head . . . I don't know about the other injuries whether before or after. I've got sort of notion that his

118

injuries were done in stages. Bit by bit.' She saw my face and said quickly, 'He probably wouldn't have been conscious . . . would have come and gone.'

I put some sugar in my coffee in desperate search of energy. 'I believe he may have managed to walk even after all that he had done to him.' I did not believe he had been attacked in the churchyard, but had made his way there.

'Oh, you can walk with a head injury. Sometimes . . . I had met him, of course.'

I was surprised. 'You had?'

'Oh yes, his wife was often in and about collecting specimens or delivering them . . . she worked in the Nuttin Research Institute down the road. It's a microbiological research centre. We help each other out on occasion, specimens, checks, that sort of thing. He collected her sometimes. That was before she drove into the back of a lorry on the M4 and killed herself. They brought her in here. We get plenty of crash victims, being so near all the motorways, but it's always a shock when you see a face you know.'

'Was she a scientist?'

'No, secretary, but she was one of those women that the whole administration depends on. Capable, you know, and hard-working, and would do anything. A bit highly strung and inclined to imagine things, but a good sort, I liked her. Pretty too.'

'And she'd lost her twin brother not long before?'

'Mm, but that was before I came, although there was still talk.'

'Oh?'

'Bit of a mystery. They thought it might be traced to a hepatitis C, rather rare.'

'How would they get that?'

Rosie smiled. 'I'm told Mrs Dryden thought she'd somehow given the infection to them, they'd been working on a vaccine at the laboratory, but it was nothing of that sort. Couldn't be, the Nuttin is very, very careful. No, they'd been on holiday in eastern Turkey so they might have contracted it there. Not her. But I don't know what the final conclusion was, I think they are still working on it.'

'But they were buried.'

'Yes, well, they have specimens,' she said delicately. 'I think the coroner left it open . . . Death from unknown causes.'

'I suppose you can usually confirm that sort of thing?'

'Yes, in the end,' Rosie said cautiously. 'Usually. Can take time. Not my job, of course. The backroom boys do that for us. We've had some real mysteries. The chap who got bitten by his ferret, and a long-running saga of this man who died with his pet rabbit. Bit of leaking kitchen equipment did for him and for bunny.'

'Your job and mine have a lot in common,' I said.

'And it doesn't do to get too close.'

'But I think you do.'

'And you.'

'Sometimes,' I said. 'Sometimes. More often than you'd think.'

'Dryden?'

I nodded. 'Yes, I didn't like seeing his face.'

'They were rather sweet together,' Rosie said thoughtfully. 'I think he was what people call a good husband,' she added wistfully.

'Must be a nice thing to have.' Or was it? One woman's good husband might be another woman's total bore.

And now he's gone and she's gone. The brother, sister-in-law, and child. The whole family group. And Chloe Devon. But there can't be any connection.

I'm not going to say that aloud, I told myself. I'll think about it later.

'Can I have some more coffee?'

'Sure.' She poured and pushed the sugar towards me. The noticing eye, I thought, doctors are trained to see that sort of thing.

120

I drank the coffee. It didn't seem to be doing much for me.

'You're too hard on yourself,' said Rosie gently.

'You work hard yourself.' It was true that her face was drawn with fatigue, but it was still a young, eager face, nothing had dented that look yet. I hoped it never would.

'True, but I get something back, and I'm not sure if you do.'

Damn that noticing eye.

'I did once,' I said. I finished my coffee. 'I'd better ring for a taxi to take me back.'

Rosie stood up. 'I'll give you a lift home.'

'Aren't you working?'

She looked at her watch. 'I should have finished three hours ago. Come on, before someone starts bleeping me. Windsor still, is it?'

'No, Brideswell now. I've just taken a house there. Is that difficult?'

'No, I know it. On my way.'

I was cold and tired, glad to sit silently beside Rosie while she drove, which she did with the competence I would have expected of her.

'To the right here,' I directed. 'Here we are.' No lights on in the house, it looked dark and empty. My spirits sagged. I needed someone to be there putting on lights and making a meal.

'Come in and let me give you a drink?' I invited Rosie.

'No, thank you. I won't. I must get home. You don't know but I have a husband and a two-year-old son waiting for me.'

Not a good husband, I speculated, as I got out of the car.

'Look after that ankle,' she said through the window. 'Who bound it up for you?'

'Dr Harlow.'

She nodded. 'I know him. He's a good chap. Bye.' She waved her hand and drove off.

I hobbled up to the door and let myself in. Everywhere

121

was dark and felt cold. I felt depressed. It would have been nice to have Humphrey here, but he hadn't obliged.

Then I heard sounds from the kitchen and his voice.

'I'm out here trying to relight the boiler.'

'In the dark?' I switched on the light. 'I thought it was cold here.'

He appeared at the kitchen door. 'Wasn't dark when I started. You can't go on living in this dump much longer.'

'I can't live in the other dump either. It's got no roof, remember.'

'Well, I've lit the fire and I have a meal ready.' He came across and kissed me on the cheek. 'You look terrible, what's up?' He gave me another and more searching look, then put his arms round me and drew me towards him. In spite of myself I resisted, feeling stiff and awkward. 'Oh, come on now, what is it?'

I told him, poured it all out to him, the relief was tremendous.

'I've never known you like this.'

'I've believed in what I was doing. Even when I was a trainee constable pounding the streets in St Andrews and Dundee, when I was sergeant in Deerham Hills, I was buoyed up by believing that I was on the right side. Not always the winning side, although I did my best to see it was, but the right side.'

'And not so now?'

'I suppose I still believe it, but I can't feel it. All I can feel at the moment is despair at the violence, the blood, the deaths. I can't see any reason for the killings in this place.'

'I think you've placed too much on reason.'

'What else is there?'

'Not much, I admit.' He drew me into the sitting room. 'But what I can offer is a hot beef casserole with what seems to be a lot of vegetables and wine in it.'

'You never cooked it yourself?'

'No, it was brought in by one Ellen Bean who said she

122

thought you would need it, and to tell you that Benjy was happy at the Midden.'

'Ellen?' I separated myself from him and dried my eyes. I was surprised to find I had been crying. 'She's probably put Happy Dust in it.' I knew what concoctions Birdie and Winifred were capable of mixing up and feeding to those they thought needed it. I could believe Benjy was happy at the Midden, he was in a familiar atmosphere.

'You're better already.'

He lit the fire in the big old grate, the ashes were still warm from yesterday. 'I've fed the cat, by the way.'

'I'd even forgotten Muff.'

'She seems recovered from whatever, judging by the way she ate. Ellen Bean brought something for her too.'

More Happy Dust, I thought, soon the whole household would be in a state of euphoria.

'Who is Ellen Bean, by the way?'

I hesitated. How to describe her? 'You know Winifred Eagle and Birdie Peacock?' They had once told him his fortune, not from his palm but from their dark green ball of glass. He had come away looking white, admitting that they had been alarmingly interesting about his past and he did not wish to dwell on what they offered him for his future. 'She's like them.'

'We'd better eat what she's given us and pray.' He disappeared into the kitchen. 'I had a spoonful and it has to be said that she makes a tasty stew.'

We ate by the fire. I had washed my hair and changed my clothes. Muff was asleep on my lap. 'Ellen didn't bring in this burgundy,' I said sleepily, sipping the wine.

'No, that came with me. My touch of witchcraft.'

Muff leapt from my lap as the bell rang. Twice.

'Oh God, I think I know who that is. He means well but I wish he hadn't come.'

Clive Barney came in shaking himself like a dog that has been caught in a shower.

'Still raining, is it?'

'Worse if anything.' He shook himself again, quite unselfconsciously. I found myself liking him more and more. But I wished he hadn't come. I knew what he was going to talk about.

Humphrey poured him a glass of wine. 'Or you could have whisky?' Or beer; I could see him assessing Barney. A beer man?

'No, I like wine.' He smiled, he had a good smile, slightly crooked but very genuine. There was an old scar on that side of his face and I wondered what had happened to him. I could find out. 'And this looks a good burgundy.'

Muff sniffed round his trousers and shoes, then leapt on to a chair near him and stared in his face. He didn't pat her head, as many might have done, or say, 'Nice cat,' but stared gravely back and then looked away. Muff appreciated that, I thought.

'I've come over to let you know what I know, which isn't much.'

'Thank you.' I was very far from being grateful, but I was sensible of his generosity in coming. He must be as tired as I was, if not more tired. He certainly looked it, and also less tidy than yesterday as if this was one day his wife hadn't pressed his tie. If he had a wife. That shirt was certainly unironed.

'The surgeon and the pathologist both had a look at Dryden. They agree: he was killed by a blow to the back of his head. A small heavy instrument. Might have had a sharp edge.'

'He survived that blow.'

'Yes, for a time, but it was a mortal blow all the same. He might never have been completely unconscious or he may have gone out like a light and then come back. Fluctuated.'

'Time?' I said.

'Within the last twenty-four hours . . . they couldn't

124

get closer . . . They agree on that estimate . . . they don't agree on the wounds.' He drank some wine. 'The police surgeon took a quick look and said they were inflicted at more or less the same time as the head wound.'

'They were still bleeding when I found him.'

'They would be, some of them were deep, and he wasn't dead . . . The pathologist says the knife wounds were later.' He hesitated, as if he didn't want to come out with the next bit. 'And were superimposed upon earlier wounds.' He looked into the fire. 'Bite marks.'

I felt sick. 'Like Chloe Devon.'

'Could be. It's something we have to consider.'

'What sort of animal did the biting?'

He shook his head. 'I suppose it might be possible to find out. If we can find out where he was attacked. It doesn't look as though he was at home.'

'You've looked?'

'First thing one of my team did. No traces of blood or violence. Doesn't look as though he'd been home for some time.'

'He telephoned me. Said he wanted to tell me something.' I don't know why I had been so slow to tell Barney.

'Did he now? Pity he never came out with it.'

'You think that was why he was killed? To stop him talking to me?'

'It could be . . . There's usually a good practical motive for the way things are done, however bizarre they look.'

'He said to me, when I first found him: "One of them was murdered." And then later: "Fire." That's what it sounded like. If that's what he wanted to say, then he said it.'

'I don't know what we can make of that,' said Barney.

'I shall be trying.'

Humphrey had kept quiet all this time, I think we had both forgotten he was there. Then he spoke: 'Is it possible the wounds were self-inflicted?'

125

'In this case anything seems possible.' He stood up. 'Better be off . . . Oh, one more thing.'

I stood up too. Here it comes, I thought. One of the reasons, perhaps the reason, for coming.

'The blood in your cellar. Seems it could have been from Chloe Devon. We'll have to have a thorough look . . . Sorry about it. Wanted you to know as soon as I knew myself. Not nice for you.'

'No, not nice. Thanks for telling me.' Especially when she had my name and address in her pocket, I hadn't forgotten that tiresome fact.

I went to the door with him and watched him go off. He looked kind of homeless. The way I felt.

Humphrey said: 'You like him, don't you?'

'Yes, more than I expected.'

I poked the fire and watched the sparks fly upward. Getting to know Barney, getting to like him, introduced complications in my life. I should have to think about it.

I picked up Muff, stroked her head as I stared into her pale eyes with their dark pupils. 'I don't want you to think, Muff,' I whispered, 'that you really understand or care about the human race. It's just a game we play between us. No, not even between us. I play and you watch.'

I don't know if Humphrey heard.

THIRTEEN

What was happening to me was frightening, but in the right circumstances might be entertainment to some. I stood outside it for a moment and viewed it: put it on the screen or between the pages of a book and it was amusement.

A murder was coming home to me. Literally, physically. Taking up a place in my own house. You can be detached about a matter when it is a professional concern, but when it gets too personal then it's as bad for you as anyone else.

Benjy had been returned late that night, looking cocky and with a note in Ellen Bean's writing, saying he had been fed and 'Didn't the ghost walk?' At least I suppose it was Ellen Bean's writing, it was certainly in her spirit.

It was no spirit message though, being in large, clear, hard handwriting. Black pen. But interestingly, it was not there in the morning. Not because it had faded but because the paper itself had suffered. Benjy or Muff. I could never pin it decisively on either, but Muff clawed papers and this was eaten. I found a chewed wet scrap by the front door. Somewhere that said Benjy to me.

I fed Muff, now apparently recovered and in rude health; I pushed Benjy into the garden and shut the door on his reluctant face. It had stopped raining but was misty and chill.

Then I went into the kitchen to make myself some breakfast. I had much to think about, both professionally and personally. But in truth I could hardly separate the two at the moment.

Now there was blood in my own backyard, I had to get out of the case. At the same time, now I was in contact with Clive Barney, it could not be me who considered the enquiry which was under way on a case of his. I must be out of that affair.

I looked at my watch. Still early. Humphrey was still asleep. Later there would be some telephone calls to make. In practice I was autonomous as head of SCRADIC, but in fact there is always a chain of command and as well as directing committees (curse their name), I had a nominal superior. He was at the Home Office because my job had various aspects, and not all of them open to the world.

To him, Lord Bixhaven, recently ennobled with a life peerage, I must report. He would have to know that I thought I should step aside from the enquiry on Clive Barney, and then I would tell him that I was taking leave. I should have to explain why that was, but he probably knew.

I fumbled my way into the kitchen to find the coffee pot. Caffeine is a drug of addiction, thank God, and one can rely on it. I usually ground the beans and had it ready the night before since I knew from long experience that my power to perform this delicate task in the morning was unreliable. And to the real addict only coffee made from the bean works the trick.

I drank a cup, black and hot, standing up with my eyes shut. When I had drained it, I opened my eyes to face the day. I had some intellectual and emotional baggage to sort out.

I took another cup of coffee back to the kitchen where I sat to drink it. The table was large, old and well scrubbed, part of the furniture left behind by Bea Armitage. I suppose one felt her presence more strongly in the kitchen than anywhere else. She must have spent a lot of

128

time there, sitting in the big chair that she had also left behind by the old Aga.

I let my mind roam, not trying to discipline it first. Names and faces darted through my mind: Billy Damiani, Chloe Devon, Bea Armitage. Somehow I saw them as a group. Then Crick and David Cremorne, Dr Harlow and Ellen Bean; the villagers. Thomas Dryden; he stood on his own with a cluster of ghostly figures behind him: his wife, his brother-in-law and his family. All dead now.

Was that what Ellen Bean had meant by the ghost walking? Ellen Bean and the Midden in Ruddles Lane ought to be visited. I liked her but did not trust her. Which, in a way, was how I felt about Birdie and Winifred in Windsor: they were like God, unknowable and unpredictable.

I forced myself to think logically, to assemble my thoughts in a pattern.

Billy Damiani had taken Chloe Devon out to dinner in Brideswell; they had quarrelled and she had left on her own. Damiani had never been totally convincing about that quarrel and the matter would certainly bear study. I counted him an accomplished liar and dissembler.

His engagement to Lady Mary was interesting. I had a private bet with myself that it would never come to a marriage: I hoped she kept the big diamond.

But no evidence, forensic or otherwise, had come up that connected Damiani with Chloe's murder or the disposal of bits of her body. He could have been in my cellar but there was nothing to show me that he had.

But for me he was high in the lists of suspects. Number One, as far as I was concerned, but that might just be personal.

But now there was another death to bring into the frame: Thomas Dryden. He, too, had been mutilated.

The bite marks linked his death with that of Chloe Devon. I had the feeling that when we found the origin of the bites, we should have the killer.

Motive? Except for Billy Damiani, since we had no names to hang upon, motive was hard to guess.

Clive Barney had said that a good practical motive would be found to be at the bottom of it. I respected that judgement, but, of course, a practical motive for a madman might not be the same as the one for a sane human being. So if the killer was unbalanced that changed the way we should think about him.

Or her. We had no indication of the sex of the killer. I used *he* and *him* in my own mind just for convenience. A matter of semantics.

One last thought had to be slotted in: what had Dryden meant with his mutter that 'one of them was murdered'? His other mutterings of what had sounded like *fire* had to be thought about but might be no more than the disconnected ramblings of a man about to die.

I found myself a sheet of writing paper upon which I began to make notes.

There was one factor that I was not going to write down: my own vibrant reaction to Clive Barney. It was irrational, unexpected, and unasked. Unreturned too, as far as I knew. It was one of those shocks that life turns up for you, usually when you are off your guard.

The smell of coffee and toast brought Humphrey down. Muff scratched the door to get out, while the dog scratched from outside to get in.

'Terrible night,' said Humphrey. 'You were tossing and turning and muttering all night.'

'I was worried.'

'I guessed that from what you were saying. Ghosts seemed to come into it.'

'Not real ghosts. Anyway, not ones that walk around with their heads under their arms and then disappear through walls.'

'Well, that relieves me.'

'No, I mean the sort that hang around in places like Brideswell. The sort that gets inside people's minds and breeds hate and revenge.'

'This isn't like you.'

'Yes, it is,' I said gloomily. 'I've always been like this underneath but I've just kept it hidden. You think because I'm more than half Scots that I'm practical and down to earth, but we're a moody, talkative, highly imaginative lot really. Driven. Think of Robert Burns, and Thomas Carlyle and James Barrie. And they're the successes, think of what the unsuccessful ones are like.'

'I was thinking more of Lady Macbeth,' he said gravely.

Our eyes met and I started to laugh.

'That's more like it.'

'I don't observe any of those truly awful traits you have called up. I think of you as a highly intelligent woman who has a very sharp notion of herself and the world she lives in.'

I looked at him.

'And who sometimes finds it painful,' he finished.

I poured us both some more coffee, and pushed the toast towards him. I had burnt the toast slightly but I usually do and I am quite used to the gently carbonized taste. Humphrey began to scrape off the burnt bits, scattering a black powder over his plate. I let him get on with it.

'There are certain practical things that follow from being personally involved.'

'Not personally.'

'Look: I knew Billy Damiani, he asked about Chloe. He involved me, whether I like it not. I should have run hard at that moment.'

'Is that all?'

'I found Thomas Dryden, he died in my presence. He spoke to me of murder. And now it seems that blood from Chloe Devon can be found in my cellar. Oh, and she had a piece of paper with my name on it when she died.'

'But you weren't living here.'

'I don't know that,' I said, desperately. 'Don't you see, I don't know.' It had been haunting me (that word again)

131

that I might have been in this house while her body or parts of it were lying in the cellar.

'I haven't helped you much, have I?'

I didn't accept that. 'Oh, it's a professional thing.'

'Clive Barney will be of more use.'

I didn't answer. It never did, I reflected, to underestimate the sharpness of Humphrey's observation.

'Have you noticed his hands?'

I had as a matter of fact: although the rest of him had been untidy last night, his hands were very clean, and well kept with neat nails.

'On both hands the first finger is the same length as the middle finger. Unusual.'

'All hands have little oddities; Tim Abbey's hands are decorated with a scar from a struggle with a Peke.' I looked at my own hands; a manicure would improve them. Perhaps now I had some time on my hands (no joke intended), I would have a manicure. And get my hair washed and cut professionally. I would telephone my own special hairdresser, an old friend and small-time crook, Beryl Andrea Barker, usually known as Baby.

He stood up. 'I have to be in London tonight. I can't ask you. One of those boring men-only dinners, but come up afterwards.'

There was no denying that Humphrey did prefer women's company to men's when he could get it. He must have many such opportunities, I reflected, on those travels of his.

'I'll think about it. Telephone you?' It was a kind of no and he knew it, accepting it with a shrug of one who has tried.

I waited until he had gone before making my telephone calls. First my secretary, then Lord Bixhaven.

His lordship listened quietly, pretending not to know what I was talking about at first, but I could tell that he had heard everything, indeed, had probably made it his

132

business to find out. It was his business, I suppose, so I gritted my teeth and got on with telling him what he already knew.

'Of course, you must have as long as you want. Rest that ankle. Awkward you being there in Brideswell, charming village, know it well.' A chuckle of false laughter. Lord Bixhaven is not really a humorous man, he uses laughter as a cover. 'Let Barney carry on and you keep out until it's cleared up. And leave the investigation on Barney himself. Cheever can chair that committee, don't you think?'

He'd had it all worked out, I thought.

Then I telephoned Rewley. I got him at last on his car telephone. 'I'm supposed to be out of it, on leave. But I'm still interested. Keep digging into Damiani, I don't like him.'

'Who does?'

'Most women,' I said.

'But not you.'

'He hasn't tried to charm me.' Or given me expensive trips to Paris and diamond rings. 'I don't trust this engagement to Lady Mary.'

'I don't think it's meant to be a permanent arrangement, is it?' asked the cynical Rewley.

'And enquire around about the Cremornes. They do own most of the village, after all.'

'Will do.' He sounded amused.

'But handle it tactfully. I don't know what underground taproots he's got fastened into the establishment and I can't afford trouble.'

Rewley did not answer this with more than a grunt. He hated having to 'handle' people but he could do it, none better.

I telephoned my hairdresser next.

'Long time no see,' said Baby chirpily. She always spoke in that way, so that I used to feel she must be permanently tuned into a 60s TV comedy show.

133

I had known her for some years and had arrested her at least once. Inside prison she had been a social success, assisting fellow inmates with their hair and advising them on make-up; even the warders were sorry to see her go. Baby emerged to take up her chosen career of hairdresser and beautician, combined with a little light crime. She had prospered in the 80s, creating a chain of three beauty clinics, only lightly mortgaged. I used to wonder what bank she was robbing.

'Now who's been looking after your hair? No, don't tell me, you've been doing it yourself. That's false economy, Char, with hair your colour you can't afford it. That russet colour can so easily go dull. Come along here and let me give you a few highlights to lift those little grey hairs.'

Baby was the only person to shorten my name, nor had she waited for permission. I booked a manicure too.

'I've got a lovely new red,' said Baby. 'Perfect for you.'

'Just plain, I think.' Nothing would convince Baby that I did not want my nails painted.

'Or there's a nice pink just come out. I could convert you to that, I think.' Beauty was an act of faith to Baby, to which conversion was always possible. 'I'll send you away looking beautiful . . . And who's the lucky man?'

That too was Baby's style. No answer was required and none given. In Baby's world there was always a man. Or, if you were that way, a woman. But always someone. For Baby herself it could be either.

We settled on a time, later that day, and then I made the call I had been working up to.

I telephoned the central HQ, identified myself, and asked for Chief Inspector Barney. He wasn't there, I was told, but might be in the Incident Room in Brideswell.

The Incident Room said he was not there either so I left a message asking him to telephone me. Then I waited.

It's interesting how guilty you can feel when only the tiniest seed of betrayal has taken root inside you.

When he rang back, taking his time I thought, I said: 'I want to ask you something.'

FOURTEEN

'I'm stepping out of things. Temporarily, of course. Leave of absence. It means I will be dropping one or two issues.'

I didn't have to say more. He knew that I meant the enquiry into his own case.

'I had heard.'

I hesitated. 'I don't know if you care one way or another, but I think you've been badly treated by even having any questions raised.'

'Thank you. I do care.'

'And if it helps, I don't expect the whole thing to go any further. I have made my thoughts clear to the powers that be.'

He was silent. I sat at the end of the telephone, clutching it to me, wondering if I had done wrong somehow. Hurt his pride, irritated him.

Then he said: 'Thank you,' quickly, in a way that reassured me. 'And what is it you want?'

'The injury to my ankle is put forward as the reason I'm taking sick leave, of course everyone knows the truth is that I am too closely involved, living here and with blood found in my own cellar.' I was talking like a book, a police manual at that. Why was I talking in this way?

He murmured something about understanding.

'I know I'm out of it, but I want to look over the Dryden house.'

Once again he hesitated. Perhaps he was a man who always thought before he spoke. But when the answer

136

came it was decided. 'Sure, of course. I'll see you get a key. Are you home now? I mean in Brideswell?'

I looked at the clock. I had about an hour before I needed to set out for my hair appointment. 'Yes, I'm here.'

'If you're still interested, there is something else about Dryden. We don't know where he was attacked, but traces of blood have been found on the paths across the fields and woods from the church and going towards the Folden road. It looks as if he came that way, falling about. Blood and skin scraps on the hedges and grass. No one admits seeing him, but it's not much used, that path.'

'I don't know it.' I was so new to the district that hardly any of the ways of it were known.

'I'll see you get a map with the key. It's not clear he knew where he was going, or if he was just wandering round in a daze. And it was very misty.'

'He got himself to the churchyard, I think that was where he meant to go.' I found myself seeing that blood-stained figure stumbling along the lanes and through the wood towards the church.

He did not ask me why I wanted the key, which was just as well since I would have been hard put to give an answer, but within me was a deep, instinctive feeling that I would know something more about Thomas Dryden if I saw where he had spent his last few days before death.

Know the victim is a sound precept for any investigator. If you know the victim, you are getting close to the killer.

I wasn't giving up investigating the murders of Chloe Devon and Thomas Dryden whatever I said aloud and in public. Clive Barney knew it as well as I did.

As if to confirm my continued interest, George Rewley came through with a call.

'What do you want first, personal or work news?'

'Personal.'

'Well, first of all: Kate's pregnant. We've discussed it for ages, but I wasn't sure if she'd be pleased when it came to it. But she is.'

'What would you have done if she'd decided she wasn't?'

'Well, with Kate, everything's a gamble.'

'I know.' But inside her was a loving heart.

'But she really loves the human race and she wouldn't kill off a member of it, especially when it belonged to her.'

I laughed. In spite of his detached tones, I could tell he was happy. And if he was happy, then it meant Kate was. It was impossible not to share her moods.

'Now the work news, please.'

His voice was amused, as so often with him. I didn't know if he found life amusing or had decided it was better to see the joke. 'I've discovered where Billy Damiani was after he left Chloe Devon and why it was hard to pin him down . . . He went straight to number seven Philadelphia Street.'

'Happiness House?' This was the name given to a quiet, expensive brothel in Soho which had never been closed down, so far. There were a lot of reasons for that, all suspect. 'It seems he's been a caller there for years. No special habits, all regular.' He was laughing. 'Anyway, that's where he was.'

I didn't ask him how he had found out this news about Billy Damiani, the police picked up lots of odds and ends of information. In this case, the Vice Squad had probably always known.

'It may explain his engagement to Lady Mary: if the story of his visits there came out, she's so socially acceptable that it might stop the laughter.'

There would be unkind laughter and to someone as socially insecure as Billy Damiani that would be worse than a prison term.

'And there's one more thing. He's booked himself into the Nelson Clinic in St John's Wood. Don't ask me why,

and doctors being what they are, I may have trouble
finding out.'

'Try. Thanks, Rewley.'

'I haven't got anything on your latest trouble in Brideswell. I wish I had.'

'There will be a result.'

'Inspector Barney's a good man. Dolly Barstow worked
with him once on a child-abuse case in Slough and she'd
said he's ace. She fancied him a bit, I think.' There was
something in his voice: I knew Rewley could read lips,
but surely he couldn't read minds.

'Clever girl, Dolly,' I said, keeping my voice neutral.
Sergeant Dolly Barstow, soon to be promoted Inspector,
was a girl I had got to know well in various cases. She
was a close friend of both Kate and Rewley.

'But she said she didn't get the response she was hoping
for.'

'I'm surprised.' Not many men could resist Dolly
Barstow when she put her mind to it.

'We're thinking of asking her to be a godmother.'

'Good idea. Dolly would be splendid. Give my love to
Kate. How's her mother?'

'We haven't told Annie yet that she's going to be a
grandmother. We haven't felt strong enough.'

'Oh, she'll be delighted.'

'Not counting on it.'

Annie Cooper, artist, was as unpredictable as her
daughter. She had been too talented and too rich for too
long. All her life. I loved her.

When Rewley had rung off, I telephoned Kate.

'I know the news. How are you?'

'Splendid, thank you.' She sounded it.

'And happy?'

'I really am, truly.' Now she sounded surprised at herself. 'I thought I might suddenly hate the whole idea, but
I don't. I even like feeling sick in the morning. It's sort
of female, somehow.'

'All the right hormones are piling in, Kate.'

139

'Oh, give me some self-will. It's not just automatic.'

Very nearly, I thought, nature is a hard act to bust. And having been that way once myself, I knew how it happened.

'You know it's only an inch or so long but it's got our name on it. And know what, I like the little creature? Already. I don't even know its sex or if it's got one yet. I must find out when that starts.'

'And you haven't told your mother yet?'

'No. But I know what she'll say: set up a trust fund at once. There's only one thing Annie respects except for top-rank art, and she has her own views on that, and it's money.'

There was some truth in that comment, but Annie was also a loyal friend and I valued that quality.

'By the way, I shouldn't let old Humphrey go too footloose for too long, he's got his admirers.'

'You've always been on his side.'

'No sides; but I recognize an attractive man and a highly desirable property.' Kate laughed and put the telephone down.

The doorbell rang. Chief Inspector Barney held out his hand. 'Brought the key round myself.'

I hesitated. 'Thank you.'

'And here is the map.'

When he had gone, I telephoned Baby to say I would be an hour late for my appointment. I put the receiver down on her protesting voice.

Then I played some music. Richard Strauss's tone poem: *Till Eulenspiegel.*

I listened to the last thrilling scream.

Music does purge the soul.

Baby pretended to be angry with me when I arrived. 'You're lucky I could fit you in.'

But anger with me was hard for her to keep up because I was so important to her. She never knew when she might

140

need me. She was so often in trouble. Baby attracted and was attracted to rogues of every sex and colour. She assured me that she had been clean for ages now, since her last encounter with a villain, but she was not to be relied upon. Trouble and Baby were twins.

She ran her fingers through my hair. 'It's a mess. You've only just got to me in time. I may be able to save it.' Having threatened me with baldness she was satisfied. 'I'll give you your manicure at the same time. On me, my treat. Good to see you, I've missed you.'

In the years I had known Baby she had not changed: she was small boned, slender with big blue eyes and hair that was sometimes fair, sometimes red, and had once been walnut dark. Today it was golden and worn in a frothy mop like a dandelion.

She settled me in a chair and beckoned to one of her assistants to do the shampoo. The girls in her salon wore pale pink tunics but Baby, being the boss, wore jeans from Gap and a personalized T-shirt with her initials on it. B.A.B.

'What about a few highlights?'

'Not my style.'

'I could make it your style. You don't do yourself justice, you know. You've got good bones, you ought to play up to them . . . You dress better than you did.'

'Thank you.'

'You could still spend a bit more. I mean you're a public figure, people know you, look at you.'

'Don't tell me I'm a role model.'

'For some girls, yes.' Baby was serious. 'Not for me, of course. There's no way you and I could ever be like each other.'

'I should think not.'

Our eyes met over the washbasin into which my hair was about to be plunged backwards and we giggled. Baby was about the only person left in the world I could giggle with now. I used to be able to giggle with my sister, but

141

once she got married she seemed to give it up. I suppose I got more serious too, life made me that way. So many dead bodies, so many lost and abused children, so many victims, and the store of laughter inside you gets eaten away.

'The trouble with you is, you need a man.' She was hovering over my dripping head with her scissors, still muttering about the need to lighten it a bit. 'You always attract such weak men, ones that want a shoulder to lean on.'

'You don't know anything about my life.'

'I can guess, can't I? And you can tell a lot from a person's roots. And I can tell right here and now that yours need nourishment.'

'And how's your life, Baby?'

She put down her scissors while her face went pink with pleasure. 'I've met such a gorgeous bloke.'

I had a passing anxiety that he might be called Billy Damiani, in many ways they were made for each other, but no, he was called Jack. He was tall, dark haired, and handsome. He was, as happened regretfully often lately, Baby admitted, younger than she was.

'But these days that's all right, isn't it? I'm in the fashion.'

'Is he a great deal younger than you?'

She was shifty about admitting how much, one decade, two decades. 'I don't dwell on it,' she said.

I was too tactful to ask what his trade, profession, or chosen villainy was. But she told me: he drove lorries across the Continent, he was one of the new Europeans, born in Hackney, brought up in Bromley, Kent, and now he had a farm in Normandy and a house in London. He belonged to the Conservative Party but never bothered to use his vote. He sounded just right for Baby.

'I do his hair,' she said. 'That's how we met, his last hairdresser had left it in a shocking state, he could see the care I took. I gave him a lovely little perm, just a

142

crop of curls, you know, all cut away, hardly there but beautiful to see, like a Botticelli angel.'

'What do you know about Botticelli?' Rudely, perhaps. I shouldn't have said it. Baby had her pride.

'I go to exhibitions,' she said, hurt. 'He's quite keen on pictures and he's teaching me.'

She had taken off a fair amount of my hair and I was beginning to get worried.

She saw my face. 'You'll be able to look after this yourself, easy for you now you live in the country.'

'How do you know I do?'

'Saw your picture in the *Windsor Evening News*. You're noticed, you know. You looked as though you had a black eye, but I don't suppose you had. Newspaper photographs never do you justice. Nasty murder,' she added conversationally. 'That poor girl.' She shook her head. 'Still, she had an accident coming to her.'

'You didn't know her?'

'I can tell you just what sort of girl she was. You learn to read looks in my business . . . Clever, sharp. She'd look out for the main chance.' A judicious note crept into her voice. 'Not real class. I feel sorry for her. I'd call her a game little bird but she'd run risks.' She looked over my head to her own face in the glass above the basin. 'Like me really. I think I'd have liked her, poor little cow.'

I could see there was a resemblance between the two if you looked at it the right way and it was like Baby to have seen it.

'How's the murder hunt going?'

I shrugged.

'Oh, it's all right, I know you won't tell me.'

'Can't, not won't.'

'And now there's been another murder.'

I was surprised. 'How do you know that?'

'On the news. Radio Reading. You don't think you're a secret, do you?'

143

'No.'

'Lively village you've got yourself too. I've got a customer from there already. I tint his hair. Lovely looking lad, dear David.'

I was interested and amused that David was vain enough to tint his hair. And trust Baby to be so admiring.

'All right, if you won't talk about the murders, let's talk about something interesting . . . The new man you've got.'

'I didn't say that.'

'You did. Or more or less. I'm good at guessing. What's he like?'

'I don't know. I'm only just discovering him. When you first meet him, you think there's nothing there at all. Later . . . you learn.'

One of the last days I had heard him talked about in the canteen over coffee. I had listened in.

'He seems so married,' someone had said. And someone else said: 'No. Not married at all. His wife topped herself.'

A man whose wife has killed herself is not a nothing. He is either a very good man or a monster. I wanted to find out which.

'I can read you like a book,' said Baby.

This was not true, I could think of many occasions, most of them professional ones, when she had certainly not read my mind, but on the other hand Baby had an uncanny knack of getting me right in personal matters.

She laughed. 'You're fishing. I can tell. One thing I do know about is women and men, and women and women for that matter. It's all the same.' She put her head on one side. 'You've never thought of that for yourself?'

'No.'

'Perhaps you're right.' She beckoned to an assistant. 'Here's Maidie, who will do your nails.' She watched me put my hand on a pink cushion. 'And that's how I know you're fishing: the manicure. You only ask for that when you are.'

144

Thoroughly unsettled by Baby, which she had intended as I well knew, she was punishing me for being an absent friend, but with clean hair and bright shining nails, I drove home.

Back in Brideswell, I fed Muff, and said a thankful prayer that Benjy was back at the Midden and that Winifred and Birdie would be back in a day or two, and then followed the road to where Thomas Dryden had lived.

It was not so far away from the Midden, I found myself walking down Ruddles Lane in the twilight. The Midden was a long low grey-stone house which faced straight on to the lane. The curtains were drawn but there were lights behind. No one looked out but Ellen Bean could probably see me in her crystal ball. There were no other houses close by, the Bean house stood on its own on the edge of a farm.

The lane rose slightly up a gentle slope at the top of which I had to take a turning to the left. A thick hedgerow lined the road on one side and a belt of old elms on the other. Beyond the trees I could see fields, a soft brown earth, turned and ready to its crops. Another field was grass with two horses standing side by side. I could smell the earth and the growing things, a green, damp smell.

There was a house standing alone in the fields; this had to be the Dryden house. The surface of the road was muddy and bore the tracks of many cars. Now it was quiet, with just one solitary police car on guard at the gate. They knew me or had been alerted by Clive Barney, so they saluted and let me go past.

One man got out of the car. 'Shall I walk across with you, ma'am?' He eyed me curiously. 'Or drive you, it's sloshy walking up there.'

'No, I'll manage, thank you.'

He didn't ask if I had a key to the house so he certainly knew that I had. 'Been crossed all day,' he said cheerfully. 'Two TV crews before breakfast. They've all peeled off

145

now. A siege in a factory in Wapping. Not our affair, that's the Met, and they're welcome.'

He watched me through the gate, holding it open for me before returning to the car.

I had changed into boots for the walk but I still wore the clothes I had worn to the hairdresser's. I felt conscious of what I was wearing. Not smart enough for Baby, too smart for a walk in the country. In my life it was hard to get the clothes right.

The house was red-brick, square and ugly. Planted down like a stranger in the English countryside about eighty years ago, I reckoned by the style and look of it, but it could last another hundred and eighty.

Why was I visiting the Dryden house? Just curiosity? A sense of possessiveness about this murder in my own backyard? Both of those things, but also the feeling that I owed a debt to Thomas Dryden, because he had tried to tell me about a murder.

One of them was murdered.

He had not had time to tell who was murdered but perhaps his house would.

I let myself in to stand in the middle of the hall. I pressed the light switch. Signs of a police team having gone over it were everywhere. Furniture had been moved, carpets rolled back and inspected for blood stains, curtains the same.

This was a shame because I could see that Dryden had kept it tidy, I liked him for that. A nice, ordinary home with clean bright paint, rugs on polished wood, and a new kitchen.

I walked up the stairs. The bathroom was new, a pale pink bath and matching everything, even the lavatory paper. Part of a fashion that had passed, but the Drydens had stayed with it. The police had been less active up here so it was tidier. A room with a small double bed and an empty feel to it. One big room with twin beds, scent and make-up still on the dressing table so this had been their room.

146

Probably her clothes were still there in the cupboard. I opened a door and yes, there they were. Tweed suits, jersey dresses, a bit of denim in skirts and jeans, a solid, professional woman's wardrobe. Size fourteen.

A pile of neatly folded nightgowns in the top drawer of the dresser, and one still tucked away under a pillow on the bed. I didn't like that.

On a table in the window were a pile of books: a word-processing manual, a dictionary of scientific words and phrases, a German dictionary, and a black folder of papers.

I opened the folder, seeing at once that it contained copies of letters and reports that she had worked on for the Institute. By the names scribbled on the top she had processed reports for more than one person. Dr Fraser, Dr James, Miss Larner. I turned them over, noting that they were dated and numbered as if they represented work in progress that might be altered. Presumably these were copies she kept for her own reference.

They were in no sort of order and some of the pages had got detached from the originals and were stuck in at random.

The clothes in the wardrobe were in order which had made me think Mrs Dryden a neat, methodical woman. But her working papers were in a muddle.

It seemed to me that someone had been looking through them. Well, I could blame that on the police. But I thought they would have left things as they found them.

Thomas Dryden, then.

I looked at the report that sat on the top of the pile. It appeared to have been heavily studied somehow. It was a report on the death of a man and his rabbit from the methyl bromide which had issued from a leading refrigerator.

This was the case Rosie had talked about.

147

Methyl Bromide.
Bromomethane Monobromomethane.

A colourless non-inflammable gas with a burning taste, odourless in low concentrations.

Methyl bromide is a vesicant. Toxic effects after inhalation include dizziness, headache, anorexia, vomiting.

I raised my head. It was clearly nasty stuff. Death could occur, and there was a period of latency.

There was more detail. 'Methyl bromide has been used as an insecticide fumigant and as a gaseous disinfectant.'

Lovely stuff, I thought.

I turned the page over. On the back there was a pencilled scribble.

Could this be how they died? I would be so relieved if they did not die from any infection that I brought back to them. I told them to get rid of that refrigerator. I did warn them. If I'd been home and not at that conference then I might have picked up what was going on earlier.

But this passage was crossed with black letters.

NOT SO. JUST MY FANTASY. GOD KNOWS WHAT KILLED THEM, I AM GRABBING AT STRAWS.

Right at the bottom of the page was a note: *Take the cat for his injection.*

I was standing there holding the page in my hands and looking out of the bedroom window when I saw the headlights of a car approaching.

The car stopped on the gravel drive and Clive Barney got out. He saw me at the window and waved.

*

148

'I guessed you'd be here.'

You knew, I thought, you enquired and they said: 'Yes, we opened the gate and she's still there.'

'Did you get what you wanted?'

'I don't know what I wanted.' I looked round the bedroom. 'I found this, though.' I handed it to him.

He read it through slowly and then again. While he was doing so I looked at Mrs Dryden's dressing table. A blonde, judging by her lipstick and powder, with a liking for sweetish scent. She had a bottle of Chanel Number 12. An old favourite of my own.

'It relates to the death of her brother and his wife?'

'It relates to her state of mind and her death. I think she was clinically depressed and her husband knew it. He'd read it more than once judging by the look of it. Meant something to him, I think.'

'Or perhaps it was the last bit of writing he had of his wife's.'

'Yes, it could be that.' I took the page away from him. 'I'd like to keep it for a while. May I? Thank you.' He was being decent. I could think of more than one reason why his investigating team might say no, but decided not to mention them. 'I'll take care of it and see you get it back. I just want to think about it.'

'The house has been swept over to see what it offers. I don't know the result yet but nothing obvious turned up. He wasn't killed here.'

'Any more blood traces on the route he might have walked?'

Barney shook his head. 'No, and it's been raining so if there was a little blood it will have been washed away . . . Nothing more as yet on your cellar. It's still sealed off.'

'Too much blood around altogether,' I said.

He knew the cellar worried me. 'If it's any comfort to you I don't believe that Chloe Dover or any part of her was in the cellar while you were in the house.'

'That's just guessing.' He was trying to be comforting.

'It's all guessing. Except for the bite marks on Dryden,

149

which may not amount to much, we don't even know that there is any connection between Dryden's death and Chloe Devon's. The lab boys can't really suggest any particular animal for the bites beyond it being small.'

He was still trying to be helpful. 'The pathologist could be wrong and I'm not putting much weight on it, but there were leaves and vegetable traces on Devon's head and shoulders, and what look like similar leaves on Dryden's clothes. The first report said geranium leaves. It does suggest that they had both been in the same spot.'

'There are geraniums all round here,' I said gloomily. 'Some in my garden.'

'Look on the bright side; it could turn out to be a rare form of the plant.'

'Is that guessing too?'

'Call it hoping.' He hesitated. He was talking to a boss figure, a powerful boss too. I was making him nervous. 'I was hoping . . . I wanted to talk things over, thought we might have a drink, or a meal . . . but you're already on your way somewhere.'

I looked at him in surprise. 'No.'

'Sorry.' He was awkward. 'But your nails. Lovely colour and you don't usually . . . Sorry, I should have said. But they look good.'

I laughed. 'Just an attempt to tidy myself up.' Damn Baby, I thought, she knew her arrow would fly.

'So? There's a lot we ought to talk about.'

'Yes, I'd like to . . . I've got to feed the cat first.'

He smiled. The smile was definitely crooked. An injury, I thought, you weren't born that way. 'I've got a dog, she's in the car as a matter of fact.'

We walked down the stairs, turning off the lights as we went. The house was quiet and dead as the two people who had lived here. A house without owners soon dies.

'Wonder what happens to this place?'

'No idea. Dryden owned the fields round here. Or had them on lease from the Cremornes. Used to farm them. Set-aside land now.'

150

'Quite an estate.'

'Small but valuable.' He sounded as if he knew. I had heard that his background was farming. 'No children. Next of kin is a sister in Australia.'

On the table was a box of papers. I had missed this box.

'The team went through those,' he said, seeing my glance. 'Household papers, bills, a few letters, nothing much.' He picked out a letter still in its envelope. 'I think he was planning to sell, this is from a house agent.'

I looked. 'Astley Green. I've heard that name before. Chloe Dover worked for them.' The envelope had no stamp. 'Delivered by hand.'

'I expect someone came over with it.'

'It could have been the girl herself.'

'I'll check.'

And so will I, I thought.

He locked the door and held out his hand for the key to the house, which I handed over. I wouldn't be going back.

From inside his car, a dark massive form stood up. His dog.

'What breed?'

He was thoughtful. 'She's a kind of a boxer.' He opened the car door, carefully, I thought, as a heavy body thudded against it making low-throated excited noises. 'She's very gentle.' He cleared the front seat. 'Get back, Emily.'

I always like men who bring their dog out on a date: it shows a nice need to be chaperoned. If this was a date.

I must stop having such flip thoughts. It was all those years with Humphrey who was so correct, so distinguished, and so bloody attractive with it. The only defence a woman had left against all those solid masculine virtues was a kind of irony.

I had the uncomfortable feeling that I was not a very agreeable person. My work ironed out some of the softer sides of a woman. But I knew I could be tender. It was still there, that capacity, it just didn't show so often.

My house was empty. I fed Muff and left a note for Humphrey. I took the opportunity as he stood by the fire in the living room to run upstairs to smooth my hair (but Baby had done a good job and the line had survived the wind and the rain) and to abandon my tailored jacket and grab a soft leather blouson.

'A drink, yes,' I said as I came back. 'A meal, perhaps. But not the Red Dragon.'

'We agree on that. I know somewhere.'

It turned out to be half a working session while we talked over the two deaths and half a quiet exploration of each other. I did not mention his wife and he did not mention my career, although both undoubtedly lurked in the undergrowth of our minds. The undergrowth in mine was sprouting fiercely, putting down strong roots and sending out feelers.

Chloe Devon and Thomas Dryden saw us through drink and the meal.

'Dryden was trying to tell me something. He knew his killer, but he was talking about another murder. "One of them was murdered," that was what it sounded like.'

'He can't have been easy to understand, poor devil.'

'No, he wasn't . . . Do you know Ellen Bean?'

'I've met the lady,' he said tersely.

'She said there was a ghost in the village. I wonder if she meant him?'

'You ask her.'

'She wouldn't give a straight answer.' Witches never did. 'I only saw Dryden three times. Once in the church-yard before I came to live in Brideswell, once again in the Red Dragon, he was very drunk, and then last night.'

I was trying to construct a person out of those three meetings.

'I wonder if he knew Chloe Devon?'

152

'No evidence, but if he drank in the Red Dragon he may have seen her there.'

'That's worth following up.'

'Perhaps he killed her then killed himself.' A Gothic thought.

'He didn't give himself the blow on the head,' said Barney seriously. 'But I'll consider him for Devon, I'm considering all the men in the village, and all the men in her life. Damiani is top of that list, but there's nothing to fix it on him.'

'Still top of my list. But he would never have done it himself. He would have paid someone.'

'Don't think I've overlooked that either.'

'And don't think I've forgotten the plodding police hours that involves.'

'Not my feet these days, thank goodness, but I have to account for them in terms of overtime and extra duties.' And, in the end, to succeed or fail.

When we came to coffee, there was first silence and then we talked to each other.

Humphrey wasn't there when I got home, not there that night at all. In the morning a weary voice sounded on the telephone.

'I'm sorry, I had to see the PM and it went on for ever.'

'Oh, sure.'

'Yes, really.'

'So what was it all about?'

'I would have told you last night, but you weren't around yourself.'

I didn't answer, no decent reply coming readily to my lips.

'I'm off to Washington and might have to drop in on Brussels on the way back, not sure for how long, but I'll telephone.'

We didn't say much after this statement, just the usual

153

this and that of two people who are keeping something back from each other. I knew what I was keeping back, so what was Humphrey's share?

After we'd finished talking, I unwound the bandage from my ankle. It was bruised and swollen, sore to touch and to walk upon. I would have to stay home today and think.

It was Achilles, wasn't it, who was vulnerable only through his heel?

FIFTEEN

Brideswell was as haunted as a village could be that night as I had slept. Later I learnt of two groups of people who were haunted.

One set because they were hiding what was not there.

The other two because they were hiding guilt that was there. At that time I had not got them identified.

And then there were some little furry creatures who were only doing what furred, toothed creatures do. Some of them were already dead because they might have been evidence. If they had spirits perhaps those little ghosts would have roamed around.

But as Ellen Bean said there was no ectoplasmic ghost, visible if voiceless, just an atmosphere of the past being too heavy to hold itself in. Persons were trying to push the weight back but it was proving too heavy a burden.

Ellen Bean said to me when we later had a private conversation (after telling me once again that she had wormed Benjy), that she now knew whose spirit was fuelling the haunting.

'At first I did not know. I sensed the feeling but I could not tell precisely where it was coming from. There is always one strong source, you know. Now I know who it was.'

Chloe Devon? Thomas Dryden?

'No,' said Ellen Bean, 'it is Katherine Dryden. She is the one doing the haunting. That surprises you, doesn't it?'

Not as much as you might suppose. I said to myself. Ellen always thought she had the answer to everything. But it is not as simple as that: she had help.

'And it is not much good asking the Rector for a service of exorcism,' she said regretfully. 'He is so modern. I'm not sure he believes in God so he is even less likely to believe in the devil.'

I am not sure I do myself, although I certainly believe in evil and have seen in sprouting out of the walls in some houses in some places.

'I think we have an infestation here,' said Ellen briskly. 'I might deal with it myself.'

Or you could call it a case of bad conscience. A communal bad conscience.

SIXTEEN

I had remembered to buy some coffee beans in Windsor market so I ground two big handfuls for my breakfast coffee. The smell encouraged me sufficiently to put some bread under the grill to toast. I knew I ought to stay around and watch it or it would burn, but as usual, I forgot and was drinking orange juice when I smelt that familiar smell of carbonized bread. It looked like charcoal. I took the bread out and started again. I would need some more bread soon, but I enjoyed going to the baker's shop.

Then I might go and see Crick and David, pick up the local village gossip and be amused by the entertaining pair. Idle the day away. I could call this break from work a holiday. Make a holiday, do the sort of thing that hardworking professional Charmain Daniels never did. Or hadn't done for a very long time.

While I was watching the second toasting, Benjy was returned to me. The doorbell rang, I answered it and a hand thrust Benjy through the gap. All I saw was Ellen Bean's retreating back. 'He's been a good boy, I've wormed him. I'm off to Reading for the day. Marketing. Tomorrow is a day on which I will not eat nor sleep.' And she was gone, leaving me with a freshly wormed Benjy and the smell of burning toast.

'Is she going marketing, boy?' I asked him. 'Or is it some witch's ploy?' There had been something about the toss of her tweed cloak that had looked determined and stylish as if she knew what she was about. 'And what's this about not eating nor sleeping?'

What I had learned from my contacts with Birdie and Winifred in Windsor was that you should never take a witch's word at face value. I wish I had the chance to call her back because I would like to have talked to her. She knew Brideswell thoroughly, and Ruddles Lane and the Midden were not so far away from the Dryden house, so the chances were that she knew more about the Drydens than some in the village and if she didn't then she could take a look in her crystal ball and get some news.

I made yet more toast standing over it this time while it browned under the grill. I ate it with honey in the kitchen while Benjy watched me. He had come back from the Beans' with several new tricks: he could sit up and beg, he could bark a thank you (I presumed it was thank you) when a piece of buttered toast was offered, and he had also, as I discovered later, learnt to walk to heel, something he had resolutely refused to master before. The only drawback was that he did not always choose to make it my heel.

I drank some strong coffee while I thought about myself. There probably was a life outside my professional world but I wasn't too sure about it. I was beginning to take the two deaths in Brideswell personally. I've often had very strong feelings about murders I have investigated, don't think I have not, police officers do, especially if a child is involved, but these feelings were different, scary.

The newspaper, the post, and the pile of notes and papers from Rewley and other sources that I had assembled on the two murders were on the kitchen table. Muff was sitting on them, purring gently. Her illness, from whatever source, was in the past. I moved her aside to look at what I had.

Two things interested me: the account of the poison, methyl bromide, preserved by Katherine Dryden and her

158

messages, comments, call them what you will, on the back.

She had been fascinated by the article on methyl bromide and played with the idea that it had killed the Beasley family. She might have talked about it. She herself had died in a motorway accident about which no suspicion of anything contrived appeared to hold. She had not killed herself nor been killed. Just one of those nasty things that happen.

But Thomas Dryden had kept this paper and, judging from the beer and coffee stains on it, had read it more than once. Who had he talked to about it? I found that worth thinking about, but I could not put a shape to my thoughts. They were swirling around. Inchoate.

And then, new fact to consider, he was going to sell the house. Well, he was unhappy, he wanted to get away. I could understand what moved him.

At this point, I could put a more positive slant on my thoughts. Chloe Devon had worked, briefly, for an estate agent. I thought it was the same one that Dryden had used.

It was a possible connection between the two murdered people, the only one I had discovered so far.

Except for the village. The place came into this somehow, I would swear. I telephoned George Rewley who was not answering but whose office answering machine was.

'Find out if Chloe Devon worked for Astley Green when Dryden put his house on their books and if they could have met. Or if she could have had any contact with Thomas Dryden.' I knew that Chloe Devon had been in this very house while working for an estate agent, but I myself had dealt directly with Mary Erskine and had not used an agent. I suppose I could ask Mary myself. 'I'd like to know if the two victims ever spoke.'

This last point was asking for magic, I thought, but I had known Rewley perform alchemy before now.

159

Then I went to my bedroom to dress before going out. It was a long while since I had kept my own house tidy. In Windsor I had regular daily help (for which I was still paying, only the lady was on permanent leave till my roof on the house in Maid of Honour Row was safe and leakproof) but here in Brideswell it was up to me again. I made the bed and dusted the room, reverting without conscious thought to the way of doing it of my younger self. My life was winding backwards.

I was dressed and ready to go out into the village when Rewley rang back. Not with any news but to find out what it was all about. He would ask Astley Green but he wanted to know why.

'What's on your mind?'

'I wish I could answer that. I'm just digging around, trying to see what connects.'

Only connect, that's what E. M. Forster said, didn't he? But he didn't have quite what I had in mind: the digging out of a killer.

'There is a connection: they were both killed in Brideswell.' He might have made a black joke about Charmain Daniels being a connection, some would, but not Rewley.

'That's a start.'

'And both seemed to have suffered similar injuries. I've heard about the bites on Dryden.'

I think everyone had, it had even leaked out to the newspapers.

Through the window I could a young woman, presumably a journalist, since she had a photographer with her, camped beneath an umbrella outside my own door.

'Yes, all of that is known, but I'm looking for something more. I want to find out if there was contact. If there was some moment when Chloe Devon and Thomas Dryden met face to face.'

'There's the Red Dragon.'

'Yes, I've thought about that and I'm on my way to ask.'

160

He didn't answer at once. 'I've nothing new on Damiani. But I can give you something on Devon.'

'Come on then.'

'I had to go back to one of the girls she worked with on Damiani's magazine, Sarah Henry, because it turned she was at college with Kate and we're asking her to dinner. Sarah relaxed a bit this time round and she said that Chloe joked that it was a good job she was a discreet sort of girl because she had something on someone in Brideswell that could blow them out of the water.'

Perhaps not such a discreet sort of girl, I thought. 'Did she say whom?'

'Not by name. But Sarah thought she'd met this person when she was working abroad.'

Could be anyone from Bea Armitage to Damiani himself, I thought. Even Nora Garden travelled. And I mustn't forget Crick and David here.

'How is Kate?'

'Fine, considering.'

'Considering what? She's all right, isn't she?' I asked with some anxiety.

'Kate is well, but Annie is turning into a professional grandmother: she has already recommended an obstetrician, a monthly nurse, and a vegetarian diet.'

'But Annie isn't a vegetarian.' Kate's mother and my dear friend, Annie Cooper, was many things but not vegetarian.

'Agreed, but she seems to think her grandchild should be.'

'Keep in touch,' I said.

The press had disappeared from outside my house when I left and the rain had stopped. I thought about what Rewley had reported of Chloe Devon as I walked towards the baker's shop. The usual crowd was there which was why I had chosen to go there first. I walked past the Red Dragon and saw a man watering the window boxes but he had the surly, withdrawn look of someone not about to answer questions willingly. I'd go in myself later, have a drink and sandwich and see what answers I could flush up. I was on holiday, not working, out of it all, but that wouldn't count.

I could feel the man looking at me as I walked away. Knows me, I thought. Wonder if I ought to know him? Since I had a large criminous acquaintance, the idea aroused thought. Hotels were usually careful about the honesty of those they employed.

Might be a murderer done his time, of course. Murderers could be very honest.

Short, sandy hair, going bald on top. Spectacles. Scrawny but with the beginnings of a pot belly. I had trained to remember faces, but no, I didn't know him.

If he knew me, then he was a face from the past. I had trained in Scotland, worked there for a very limited time, then moved south to in Deerham Hills in Hertfordshire, then briefly to London, to the Met, and at last to a unit in Windsor. I had moved a lot and in this professional progress I had run across plenty of unpleasant people.

Nora Garden was there before me in the baker's, choosing her loaf. She must get up early, so she was probably not working. I hadn't seen her on the television screens lately. I wondered how she made out. As she had said herself once: there wasn't much work around for actresses of her age. 'Get to be ninety and a Dame of the British Empire,' she had said, 'and I'll be working all the time.'

Today she was sorting over the wholemeal rolls looking for the ones that were slightly burnt, which she said improved the flavour. The baker's wife, born a Beasley, married to a Beasley and there must be a good deal of inbreeding in the village, looked on patiently.

'We could always burn a batch specially for you, Miss Garden,' she said. 'But you'd have to take the whole lot.'

'No, thank you, dear, just go on burning a few as usual,' said Nora equally straightfaced. 'I'll take four.'

162

She turned round and saw me. 'Hello, and good morning. How are you?' She looked down at my ankle. 'How's it doing?'

'Healing.'

She waited while I bought a loaf, selected some brioches, and picked out some iced biscuits, before saying: 'Bad day. I know about Thomas Dryden.'

It was all over the village by now I supposed. If she only just knew, then she was one of the last to hear.

'I was learning a script yesterday, didn't go out. Used to walk the churchyard sometimes, learning my lines. Not yesterday, though. Glad I didn't now.'

All right, I thought, no need to explain yourself. No one is suspecting you.

'He was a nice man,' said Mrs Beasley. 'Till he took to drink. And that wasn't his fault, he was upset about his wife. And even then he was a gentleman.'

'Agreed,' said Nora.

'This used to be a nice village once,' said Mrs Beasley. 'Now I don't know what to make of it, nothing but terrible deaths.' She looked at me as if it was my fault.

I paid her and left the shop with Nora. David Cremorne was outside with his shopping bag. I couldn't help giving a quick look at his hair which I now knew to be tinted. It looked natural, with a beautiful cut. Baby and her minions had done a good job.

'Nora, Charmian, lovely to see you both,' he said. 'Crick's on his cooking stint today, so I'm on the marketing shift. I'm better than he is at both, but he has to have his turn or he sulks.'

'He can come and cook for me any day he likes,' said Nora.

David turned his attention to me. 'You've lost weight.'

'Oh, good.'

He was scrutinizing me. 'Or is it just your expression . . . thoughtful, anxious. You look haunted.'

Haunted, that word again. I was looking for a

murderer, that's what my look was. 'How's work?' Shift the subject away from me and my look and haunting. 'The book?'

'The old one is selling in a modest way. But I am well into my new one. Lord Curzon. I've mentioned it, haven't I? I talk about it a lot. A marvellous man and much underrated. All that circle: A. J. Balfour, Lady Elcho, the Grenvilles, the group of friends who called themselves the Souls, fascinating. And both his wives, his daughters, all so vital and interesting. Oh, yes, I know I can make something of it.'

He sounded keen, happy.

'But what I shall live on while I'm doing it, I don't know. I think I shall apply to the Society of Authors for a grant.'

'At least you've got that lovely house to live in,' said Nora. 'Often fancied it myself, but it always goes to one of the family.'

'Yes, aren't we lucky?'

Carrying my purchases, I turned back to my own house, it was in my mind to drop in at the Red Dragon, take another look at the sandy-haired man, and ask a few questions about Chloe Devon and Thomas Dryden.

But a glance towards my house changed my mind.

The two journalists had gone but there was a small, battered Ford Cortina outside my gate. I knew this to be Lady Mary's, but when she got out of the car to hail me, I had never seen her dressed more elegantly and more expensively.

'Hello,' she said. 'Thought I'd just drop in.'

'Come in.' I walked up the path ahead of her. 'Not sure if my house is grand enough for those clothes.' I ran my eyes over her: Caroline Charles suit, Ferragamo shoes, and the bag looked genuine Hermes. It all added up to several thousand pounds' worth. Lady Mary always had charming clothes, usually unpressed, but this was above her usual standard. Her hair too, cut and set by a master. 'You look lovely.'

'Oh, I know where to shop when I've got the money.'

'And have you got the money?'

'Not yet.' She smiled. 'But my credit is good.'

I surveyed her. Clothes, hair, scent, perfection. 'What are they in aid of?'

'Going to see Billy's mother,' she said, stroking Muff.

'Never imagined he had one.'

'Oh, he has. Coming over from Paris. That's where she lives. And then I'm taking him to meet my grandmother. He's looking forward to meeting a countess.'

'He's out of the Nelson Clinic then?'

She looked surprised. 'Yes, how did you know about that?'

'I heard.'

'You must be keeping an eye on him.'

'Just interested.' I studied her face. 'Ill, was he?'

'No.' She looked embarrassed. 'He's one of those people who thought you ought to have a check-up when you're getting married. I expect he'll want me to go for one too.'

Terrified of AIDS, I decided sardonically.

'Are you serious about this marriage, Mary?'

'I'm serious about his money,' said Mary grimly.

'Oh, Mary.'

'Don't pretend to be shocked. You're not really. I'm twenty-eight and I want a household and children.' She said it in that order and meant it that way. Husband came last. It had not always been so, she had loved her soldier boy.

Muff leapt down from her lap. 'After all, you're not above a bit of jilting yourself.'

I didn't answer. But I presumed she was making a sharp comment on the Barney versus Humphrey contest, if she wasn't just guessing, and I wondered how she knew.

'Of course, if you'd like to swap me Humphrey,' she said, 'I might do a trade.'

I felt a bit sorry for Billy Damiani. I also wondered

165

what she meant and if she was indeed hinting at Clive Barney.

But no, it was just one of her flip remarks, she couldn't know about him, there was nothing *to* know. She always fancied Humphrey and he liked her. They might have made a thing of it if I hadn't come barging along. He was more out of her social drawer than I was. I wouldn't use the word class but its principles still operated in the world they moved in.

Mary was not a hard nor a mercenary person so that there had to be a reason for her behaviour. I supposed I would learn why and how in the end.

'Anyway, I came to see you.' She sat down in the chair by the window. 'This room will look good when you've got a bit more furniture,' she said absently. 'It's changed since you took over. For the better, really, much as I loved Bea she wasn't a home maker.'

She paused. 'I'm trying to think how to put it: I am Bea's executrix. You know that. She didn't have a lot of money but over the last year she seems to have had a lot less. It's been melting away.'

'How much?'

'About sixty thousand. Not a fortune.' Lady Mary had rather grand ideas about what constituted a fortune. 'But it was more or less all she had.'

'So what did she do with it?'

'No idea. It was liquid cash, in Coutts bank. She drew it out in three instalments.'

'And nothing to show for it? Jewellery, pictures?'

Mary shook her head. 'No, but a conversation I had with her gives me the idea that she might have lent it. She said to me once that the best way you could show friendship to anyone was to help them out when they needed it. I think that's what she did.' She paused. 'But I believe she wanted it back. She was realizing that she might need full-time nursing care and that costs. Bea needed her money for herself.'

166

'Ah,' I said thoughtfully.

She saw my face. 'She didn't lend it to me.'

'No, of course not.'

'Well, it crossed your mind.'

'I suppose I wondered why you came here to tell me this.'

'If you're going to be like this, I shall wonder myself.'

'Mary, come on.'

'Bea's last years, her last months, were very circumscribed. Narrowed. I think all her close friends were here, in Brideswell.'

I was thinking. 'Any names?'

'Nora Garden, Crick and David, and Dr Harlow.'

'Harlow?'

'Yes, she got very close to him, as she and her cat got older. She relied on him a lot.'

'But it was a professional relationship.'

Mary said softly. 'She was old and had always liked attractive men . . . he's that . . .'

'I thought you liked all these people,' I said.

'I do, each and every one, but this loss of Bea's money is worrying and I want to know where it is.'

'She didn't give it to Billy Damiani to invest?'

'She did not,' said Mary forcefully. 'That remark is beneath you. Billy's no angel, goodness knows, and I'm not sure how he made his money, although I expect I shall find out, but he did not take Bea's thousands.'

He might be a murderer but his money was real, that's what Mary was saying.

'And he didn't kill Chloe Devon,' said Mary, reading my thoughts.

'He might have done.'

'I won't ask if you have any evidence or if it's just prejudice, but I guess you don't have anything real against him.'

I didn't argue with her. 'So what are you doing about Mrs Armitage's missing money?'

167

'Well, I'm going to be looking. There's no record, letter or receipt. I think Bea would have had one, she might have been generous, but she wasn't stupid.'

'Did you ever hear Chloe Devon saying anything about having interesting information about an inhabitant of Brideswell?'

'Can't say I did, but I hardly spoke to the girl. Bea said something on those lines once. But she laughed when she did. She liked whoever it was and whatever she meant.'

'The person she lent her money to?'

'Could be.' She frowned. 'Chloe saw me with you once and asked who you were. I told her. I think she knew but wanted it confirmed.'

'Did you give her my address?'

'No.'

But she could have found out easily enough that I was interested in the house in Brideswell, she knew the house agency game.

'She had my name and address on her,' I said.

'I thought at the time she might have wanted to talk to you. Perhaps she did know something.'

We sat for a moment in silence, then Mary removed Muff from her lap and Benjy from her feet and stood up. 'Well, that's it. I wanted to tell you about Bea's money.'

I waited. More was coming.

'I thought you might be able to recommend a private detective that I could use.'

'I expect I could. But I should think your solicitor might be able to help there.'

The telephone rang. For a moment I thought of ignoring it.

Lady Mary moved towards the door. 'I'm just going. Take your call.'

'No, wait a minute, just in case.'

Mary nodded, her face alight with curiosity.

It was Rewley. 'Briefly, the answer is yes.'

168

'So, while Chloe Devon worked for Astley Green she did meet Thomas Dryden about his house,' I said.

'I could have told you that,' said Mary from the door.

'But you didn't . . . nothing, Rewley, talking to someone else.'

'After Bea died I put the house here in Astley Green's hands. I used to go to dancing classes with young Astley . . . Before I thought about you.'

I gave her a little push. 'Be quiet, Mary, I can't hear what I'm being told.'

'What you're being told,' said Rewley, 'is that she continued to do odd work for them even after she'd started working on Damiani's art magazine. And she did come out to Brideswell to view a house that the owner was considering selling.'

'Dryden?' I said.

'Yes.'

'So they met, and we shall never know what they said to each other. But it's a link, isn't it, a connection, between the two murder victims.' I looked at Mary, standing half in and half out, letting the door swing. 'Do you know anything about it, Mary? Anything at all?'

She shook her head. 'No, but if I think of anything, of course, I'll say.'

I could hear Rewley murmuring something. 'I've just seen a first forensic report on the blood and remains in your cellar.'

'Remains?'

'It seems there was something of that too . . . The plaster was scraped off and traces of skin and bone were found in it as well as blood.' So Chloe Devon had been there.

Mary was trying to read my face. She was staring at me intently.

'They can't tell if the girl was killed in your cellar, cut up there, or the corpse just stored there before getting distributed around the place.'

169

'What a horrible, blunt way you have of putting things.'

Mary must have been able to hear what he had said, or else she could read my face, because I saw the colour drain from her cheeks and she swayed.

'I must go now, Rewley, no more details just yet.' And I banged the receiver down. And I rushed to put my arms round her. Distantly, I had just heard his voice talking about animal blood and something . . .

I knew it was important, but I knew I could not listen now. He seemed to be saying something about disinfectant.

'So what's it all about?'

I had her lying back in the chair, with the colour coming into her face. 'You nearly fainted just now.'

'I never faint.'

'You came pretty close to it . . . Could you hear what Rewley was saying.'

'Bits. Enough.' She sat up. 'Sorry, it was stupid of me. I used to play down there as a child when I stayed with Bea. It seemed a kind of magical place. I suppose there were rats?'

'Not rats,' I said.

'And it made me sick to think about it at that moment. No, I would have known if there were rats. I remember David and I made a sort of house down there.'

'I didn't know you knew David as a boy.' I should not have been surprised because I knew well that people in Mary's social class seemed to know each other from babyhood onwards. All related by generations of intermarriage. They formed a closed and golden circle.

'Child, he was quite little, he's younger than me. He was with his mother then. It was just that one summer. I'd almost forgotten it . . . But it came back with a rush. And I remembered . . .' She stopped speaking.

'Remembered what?'

'I remembered that we played a game we called Prisoners, about people being shut up down there, like a dungeon.' She swallowed. 'Surely nothing we did, nothing we played . . .'

Could their child's play presage the future, she was trying to say.

'I'll get you some water.'

I stood thinking by the old stone sink no one could accuse Bea Armitage of having the modern touch, the sink was an archeological relic, while I waited for the water to run really cold. We had good sweet water in Brideswell.

'Here you are,' I said, handing her the glass. 'Nothing that children do carries on into the future.'

A soothing lie: the other side of that coin was that the child is father to the man. Or so the saying goes.

SEVENTEEN

Whatever I may have said to Mary (and she had gone away happier, but there was still something there that I did not like), I thought the past could weigh on the present and pretty heavily at that.

I had no doubt what I was going to do. This wasn't my affair, officially I was on leave, out of it all, but life had dragged me back in. Or death itself, if you preferred to put it that way. Thomas Dryden himself had engaged my attention. I owed him something.

'One of them was murdered,' he had said.

Or that was what it had sounded like, and I was still thinking about it. Then he had muttered odd words in the ambulance: I did not understand what he had meant by those either. But they were there in the back of my mind all the time.

I closed the door behind me and walked through the village street. I realized that I had barely known Brideswell under normal conditions. Murder had marked it out for its own all the time I had been there. All the same, a number of ordinary villagers, who perhaps felt untouched by the deaths, were walking the streets on their way to shop or post a letter or buy a newspaper. I already knew that many of the villagers commuted to work in London, Reading, or Oxford, so they were away but they had left their spouses at home. Not as many as there would have been once because most of the couples worked. You had to have a good income to afford to live

172

in Brideswell and for many people that meant two incomes were needed. So there were not as many women about with shopping baskets as there might have been once and not many children. But Brideswell had several excellent schools so I had to imagine that the children were safely tucked away within the walls of the Abbey School, Fountains, and Mrs Berkeley's Playgroup, 7 Church Passage. There were usually shouts and music coming from Church Passage so I knew her group was flourishing.

I wondered how Ellen Bean was getting on at the Midden. She had never asked me inside, obviously you had to be either an animal or a witch to get hospitality. I must ask Birdie and Winifred about her, they would give me an honest view of her character. They were sharp-eyed ladies with few illusions.

But I wasn't visiting Ellen today, she could wait, although I remained interested in those ferrets with their sharp teeth.

The Red Dragon was open, but empty of customers. It smelt of brass polish and beer which, oddly enough, made a not unpleasing combination. The barman was rubbing a glass with a white linen cloth.

I approached him. 'You know who I am?'

He nodded silently. Certainly he knew. It was part of his job to know who was who and it was a part he enjoyed.

'So you also know what I am.' This was a statement and not a question. 'I want to ask you a few questions.'

He stopped rubbing the glass. 'Is this official?'

I shook my head. 'Not exactly.'

'Not exactly . . .' He savoured that. 'Boss doesn't like us talking to the police.'

'You remember the girl Chloe Devon?' He nodded. 'And you knew Thomas Dryden . . . Did you ever see them talking?'

'He bought her a drink once. Not a come on, or any-thing. I got the idea he'd met her before . . . might have

173

been over selling his house. They seemed to be talking about it. Sounded like that.'

'Yes, it might have been about a house,' I said.

'Sounded quite harmless.' His eyes challenged me: 'Go on,' he was saying, 'tell me it wasn't so harmless as all that. Tell me I've handed you a gobbet.'

The sandy-haired man appeared from behind a door as I left. He had been waiting for me. He touched me on the arm.

'You don't remember me?'

'No.'

'You ought to. You put me away.'

'I did?' I was searching my memories. 'What for?'

'Murder. I did life.'

'Who did you kill?'

'My wife. It was a domestic murder. Almost justified, the judge said.'

I was remembering him now, my first murder case, and I had got a conviction. Not a nice murder at all, in spite of what he had said. I could see the sneaky little rat-face of the young man he had been.

'How long have you been out?'

'Good time now. Put it all behind me,' he said virtuously. 'Wouldn't talk about it now but for seeing you. The guv'nor here knows all about it, of course.'

I nodded.

'I've married again.'

I wasn't surprised, of course he would marry again, might even murder again. I wondered if he'd told her about her predecessor and what had become of her, and what his present wife thought about it.

'Sharp, you were then,' he said breaking into my thoughts, his voice admiring. 'I only made one slip, and you were on to it at once.'

Clever young me, I thought. I was remembering it myself now. Money came into it, naturally.

'Yeah,' he went on. 'I told you I wasn't short of money

and didn't need her insurance money, but I'd got a garage half-built and hadn't got the money to finish it. You caught on to it, straight away.'

'Got a car now, have you?' I said thoughtfully.

'No, my wife doesn't like them, says they aren't safe.'

He said it without a smile and I swear he was not making a joke.

'Sensible woman,' I said.

Crick and David lived in their beautiful house in a state of dignified disorder. The furniture came with the house, David had told me on my first visit, but the books and the muddle are ours. But the brass knocker on the door was beautifully polished and that was David's work because I had seen him at it.

Crick opened the door to me, throwing it wide and greeting me with a generous shout of welcome. 'Come in, come in.'

Behind him I could see David at work at his desk. He wrote in longhand on sheets of bright yellow paper. A typewriter was on the table behind him. But David had a neat pile of yellow pages at his right hand. The life of Lord Curzon must be going well.

I walked in. David stood up, smiling his open welcome. The desk at which he had been working was a nice plain piece of late-eighteenth-century carpentry. It was small, and possibly it had been made for a woman, but David looked comfortable at it. He held out a hand. I couldn't help remembering how welcoming they had been to me.

'How's the ankle?'

'Much better. But I'm taking a bit of time off.'

'But still worrying about the murders,' said Crick, drawing a chair forward for me.

'What makes you say that?'

'I could say I could read it in your face, but in fact I saw you with the other policeman. You looked serious.'

'It's a serious business.'

175

'Who's laughing?' said David.

'Let me get you a cup of coffee.' Crick was bustling round. 'We're just having one.'

I accepted a cup gratefully. Their coffee was famous. 'You must have known Dryden quite well.'

'Only by sight,' said David.

'Not well,' said Crick almost at the same time.

I sipped my coffee. 'You didn't know him as a boy?' I looked at David who looked blank.

'No.' He stood up. 'Let me get you some more coffee. We pride ourself on our brew. Crick's brew really, he's the coffee-maker always.'

'This is delicious coffee, Crick, how do you make it?'

'I put in a pinch of cardamom . . . learnt that trick in the Lebanon. In the old days,' he added hastily. 'And I always mix my own coffee beans. Ring the changes, you know. I shop in Oxford market . . . or Wellington Yard if I'm in London.' He took it more seriously than I thought I could ever manage to do.

'I must learn. I came round to ask you if you'd have dinner with me one night. Might make a little party of it. Ask Mary.'

'And her betrothed?' said David. A little sourly, I thought.

'Couldn't leave him out.' Unless he was under arrest for murder, of course.

I was discovering that one of the disadvantages of not being officially engaged in an investigation was that I could not come right out and say: 'And did you ever borrow any money from Bea Armitage?'

And even if I did so now, then they might retort: 'And what is it to do with you?' Adding, if they retained their presence of mind: 'And what connection is this with the murder of two people?'

'She's the executor of Mrs Armitage's will.'

'I don't suppose she had much to leave,' said Crick.

'No, so Mary said. Not much at all. Money seems to

176

have melted away.' I took another sip of coffee. 'Mary thinks Bea was too generous with her money.'

I had come as near as I could to asking directly if Bea Armitage had given or lent them money.

The two men exchanged a look. They had understood me only too well, that look said.

Crick said deliberately: 'Bea was very kind and generous to us when we came here. But not with money. She gave us enormous support. Of course, she knew how hard up we were. How hard up we are, everyone does.'

I managed a smile. 'She was a marvellous lady. I can feel it in the house. I hate the way the cellar seems to have been used.' I finished my coffee and stood up to go. 'You must feel the same, David, more so really.'

David looked at me. 'Oh?'

'Mary said you used to play there with her.'

David helped me on with my coat. 'Don't remember that.' And then as he settled my coat on my shoulders, he said: 'Yes, I think we did kid around a bit.'

'Funny how you forget things,' said Crick. 'Mind how you go with that ankle.'

Then I left, and I heard them close the door firmly behind me. As I walked away I realized that I had just alienated the two people who had been my first friends in the village.

And we hadn't finalized the arrangements for dinner, either.

But I had learned something. When David had spoken about not knowing Dryden well and not remembering playing with Mary in the cellar when they were children, I had recognized that tone and that look.

Something false. I did not believe it.

I went back to my own house and let myself in to confront a morose cat and a dead fire. I sat thinking.

Why lie?

Children did forget things. The play had meant more

to Mary than to David, she had remembered and he had not. But then he had pretended that he had.

Lies are tiresome things, they remind people of other lies. And you ask yourself why? Or you do if you are a person like me. Trivial lies like this one are the most puzzling of all.

They make you wonder what other untruths have been told. A child's fibs might mean anything, might mean nothing. David was no longer a child.

I found myself thinking about his hair. Another trivial, cosmetic lie. It seemed to me that Beryl Andrea Barker was more responsible for that hair than nature. I suppose the thought had been at the back of my mind for some time, gradually working its way to the surface as buried things will.

I was not allowing myself to confront why it mattered so much, but I could hear Thomas Dryden muttering that one of them was murdered.

If he didn't mean his wife or the Beasley family, and was not referring to Chloe Devon (and it would be a strange way of talking about a girl so openly and terribly murdered), who then was the victim?

Only one death left to consider: Bea Armitage.

There it was, I had got that thought formed and into the open. I could look at it now and consider it.

Had Bea Armitage been killed, and if so, in what way? A way that had passed for natural death. Her doctor had said so, it seemed. I might ask about that.

But had I an intellectual need to connect it with David and his fibs?

I knew the person to ask about his hair and she would be delighted to talk. She'd be there in her shop, checking the stock, keeping an eye on her assistants, flattering the clients. Baby loved her job.

And all the time she would be giving herself little glances in the wall mirrors and smoothing her hair and thinking about her lipstick.

178

Baby did not answer the telephone herself. It was her pride that she had assistants who would call her.

'Hello? Did you want to speak to me?' She was probably polishing her nails as she spoke. Of course, she had assistants to perform that service for her now as well. Perhaps she was just stretching out her hand on the little cushion while a new colour was painted on. There always was a colour on her nails. I had wondered if there was much nail beneath it after all these years, or only layers and layers of enamel.

'Baby?'

'Ah.' That gave her a clue. I was one of the few women left outside prison who called her by that name. 'Ah, it's you again. What is it now? Hair not right? I'm telling you that you ought to brighten it up. Owe it to yourself.'

'No, it's not my hair, I'm pleased with it.' I realized with surprise that I was, that I liked the way it made me look.

'Oh, good. What then? Because I'm really busy.'

'I wanted to ask you something.'

'You ask me?' She sounded genuinely surprised. She was clearly running over the subjects on which she was an expert: petty crime, hair, and women covered that field.

'It's about hair, but not my hair. Your other customer from this village . . . you touch up his reddish hair?'

'That's right. He only comes in occasionally to have the odd touch-up. I think he goes to Alfredo in Knightsbridge for the main job.'

'I thought it might be the case.' I could hear her talking to someone in the salon. She seemed to be soothing an irritated customer. 'Are you listening, Baby?'

'Yes, I'm listening, but get on with it, I'm running a business here.' She loved saying that. Being the important successful woman of affairs talking to Charmian Daniels who was just a police officer.

'Well, could you make a guess what the colour of his hair truly is?'

179

'I don't have to guess, dear, it's black. Or a very dark brown. You only have to look at his eyebrows to know that. People with really red hair have pale red eyebrows. Eyelashes too. Sometime they dye them. His are not dyed. I can tell the difference.'

'I knew you'd be able to. Thanks, Baby.'

'Any time . . .' She got her revenge. 'But easier after four o'clock, not so busy then.'

It was hard to get the better of Beryl Andrea Barker, but inside she bled like everyone else. I knew it and she knew it. She still mourned for her lover who had died. Been killed, in fact. Only not by Baby who was many things, indestructible being one of them – but not a killer.

'Let's meet sometime, Baby,' I said. 'Let's lunch.'

'Yes, sure.' She was surprised. She would never believe she could be a support to me.

I hesitated, then said: 'You've met all sorts inside.' I meant she'd lived in the same prison as some very violent offenders, never mind if they were women. 'What's the strongest reason for murder, in your opinion?'

She didn't have to think. 'Oh, sex, for sure. Either jealousy or fear of losing someone.'

'Not money?'

'Oh, well, that could come into it, couldn't it? If you lose money, then you might lose the person you loved.' She spoke with a sad knowledge of the world she lived in.

'So it's sex and money?'

'Not just sex, Char,' she corrected me. 'Love, I prefer to call it love. It's very strong.'

'And what about revenge?'

'Well, it would be revenge for sex or money, wouldn't it? Probably, anyway.'

That was Baby, I thought. Murder for her would always be something created between the sheets with an eye on the bank balance.

'Of course, there are those who seem to do it for fun, although I haven't known many of those, women don't do things that way so often. Though I did know a kid, she killed that way, pretty little thing too.' She paused and thought about it. A waste of prettiness it had been. 'But I suppose even there you could call it sex. Or they hate the human race, and want revenge.' Baby could be very articulate when she wanted. Behind her the hairdressing salon was rattling with noise and life. Someone had switched on the radio, a popular music programme. 'You haven't got one like that on the books, have you?'

'No, I don't think so. Can't be sure, but I think not.'

'Glad to hear it. Now let's have that lunch. I shall take you up on that. And bring along that new man of yours.'

'Don't go on about that, Baby.'

'Bound to be an improvement on the last one.'

'You don't know anything about him.' I protested. Poor Humphrey.

'No, but I know you.' She laughed. 'You do give yourself away.'

She was still laughing when I put the telephone down. I had enjoyed my conversation with her, and I had used it to let her observations about David's hair colour settle down and make a shape in my mind.

Some such shapes are worse than others and this was a bad one. David dyed his hair from black to reddish gold. A lovely colour but I didn't think he did it from vanity. I did not judge him to be a vain man. Not in that sort of way.

I sat there thinking while the fire died down into ashes. Why did David tint his hair?

Is it because he doesn't have the naturally red hair of the Cremorne family?

But why should that matter?

Let us suppose that he is not a real Cremorne. Let me suppose further that the real Cremorne boy whom Mary had played with did have red hair but died.

All right, why should David pretend to be what he is not?

There was an easy answer to that one: because he and

181

Crick get a lovely free house to live in. Nothing matters so much to David as his writing, but he does not earn real money from it. He needs the freedom the house in Brideswell gives him.

Bea Armitage may have picked up the deception. Add to it, that she may lent the two of them money and you had an explosive mix.

I made up the fire, put a guard in front of it in case of sparks (I was learning about wood fires), took my coat, and went out again. It was raining hard by now.

Crick opened the door to me. I didn't wait to be asked in, I just went in.

There was a suitcase in the hall and other signs of packing. They had got on with it fast.

'Going away?'

Crick said nothing. His eyes looked dark and anxious.

David came through from the back of the house. 'What is it?' He saw me. 'Oh, it's you.' He had his arms full of papers.

'Going away?'

The two men looked at each other. 'Just tidying up,' said David. He was always the stronger of the two, I thought.

'Something more than that, I fancy. What would you say if I asked to see your passports?'

'They're in order,' said David.

'Oh, sure. But that's not the point, is it. What names do they bear?'

Crick went to stand beside David. 'What is it you want?'

'I want to talk to you. Both of you. Let's go in and sit down. Don't bother about any coffee this time, Crick.'

'I wasn't going to.'

I led the way into the living room, they followed me silently. I sat down. They both stood there looking down at me. Tall men, nearly the same height, David was slightly the taller. The younger generation usually is.

182

'Your hair is a nice colour, David,' I said. 'I've always admired it. Autumn Bronze, that's the shade you go for, isn't it? I've got a hairdresser in Windsor too.'

'What's this about?' said Crick quickly.

'Let me tell you a story. Let's suppose there are two men. Perhaps father and son. Or it could be a sexual relationship.'

I heard Crick give a kind of growl.

'All right. I'll accept father and son. Easy to check, anyway. So we can leave sex out of it and put love in.'

David started to protest: 'Look here—'

I didn't let him. 'Stop it and listen to me. Let's suppose the elder man has been married twice and has a son by the first marriage. This second wife already has a son, a true Cremorne. This son dies in Italy. His wife is already dead. This man's own son is very talented but they have no money. Or very little. But they can use the Cremorne connection to get a free house while David – yes, I have to name you – gets on with writing. There's not much danger of being found out: the Earl is generous to his own family and out of the way. Not generous to outsiders, of course, so it wouldn't do to get found out. How does that sound?'

Neither of them answered.

'I think Bea Armitage found out. She guessed. She had known the real David Cremorne as a boy.'

Suddenly Crick said: 'Bea knew straight away. She laughed, she would never have said anything. Bea Armitage was a good, kind, loving woman.'

I just looked at him.

'I would never have hurt Bea.'

I did not answer.

'Besides . . .'

'Besides what? Besides, Chloe Devon knew too?'

'Oh, God,' said David. 'Don't say it.'

'Chloe Devon knew, she possibly found out in Rome. She didn't think it was a joke.'

'You're getting this wrong.'

'And did Dryden know too? She could have told him, they did meet . . . Are you going round killing everyone who knew?'

David sank down and put his head on his hands.

'Scream if you want to,' I said.

EIGHTEEN

The room seemed drained of air as if I had exploded a bomb which had sucked out the oxygen. I could see David breathing very fast, taking in great gulps of air. For myself I felt cold and calm.

I had no sense of personal danger although I knew it could be there. But I was careful to position myself near the door and facing them.

Crick said: 'You cannot believe that we would kill two people so brutally for any such relatively unimportant reason. All right, we might be acting a lie because it suited us, but it wouldn't be worth killing for. We could pack up and go. And did you really suggest that Bea Armitage came into it? That she might be a victim too? We loved her, if you know what that means.'

I stood silently observing the play of emotion on his face. 'I think you might have killed Bea Armitage, although I don't as yet know how. From that death, the rest follows.'

'No one killed Bea. It's monstrous what you are suggesting. You think we are monsters.'

'I've known people kill for less,' I said.

David stood up. 'I don't know whether to laugh or cry. You are out of your mind.'

'I've heard people say that too.'

'We're not getting across to you, are we? We have not killed anyone.'

'I liked you,' I said. 'Admired you both.'

The front doorbell rang. Two loud peals.

David looked at me and shrugged. Neither man moved.

'The police?' said Crick. 'Your colleagues?'

The doorbell sounded again.

'It's your door,' I said. 'You open it.'

Crick went to the door. I heard him laugh. Ellen Bean came in smartly. 'You took your time.'

'We didn't feel exactly free agents,' he said.

She looked from face to face. 'Oh, I know where you're at. You've found out who David is. Or who he isn't.'

I was no longer in command of the situation. It was getting away from me.

'How long have you known? Don't tell me you picked it up in your crystal ball?'

She laughed. 'I've always known. I've known since I first set eyes on him. Half the village knows.'

David made an inarticulate noise. Ellen gave him a smile. 'Well, all the old-timers that is. Not that I'm one of them, but I'm a good guesser. Ask the real villagers who've lived here all their lives. They know a Cremorne when they see one. Or when they don't.' Her smile was broad and toothy like the smile of small crocodiles.

'You haven't lived here all your life,' I said, remembering what I had been told.

'Not lived here, not as an adult,' said Ellen, switching the smile my way. 'But I stayed here with Auntie as a kid. I played with the boy that was David and this wasn't him. Knowing is knowing, you don't forget. There's a feel about people and nothing changes that.'

'Why did no one say anything?'

'Why should we? Not our business if he wanted to pretend to be a boy that was dead.'

'You knew that too?'

'Course I knew.'

'You know too much.'

'So I suppose you are now accusing him of murdering Chloe Devon because she knew about it too?'

186

I looked at her thoughtfully. 'You know, you can be really annoying.'

'It's just because you don't like the truth.'

'Is it the truth?'

'Yes, without doubt.'

'Now don't go on about the varieties of truth there are,' I said irritably.

'You are in a paddy.'

Crick broke in. 'Of course, Bea knew who were and who were not. She just laughed.'

'What's your real name?' I asked the other one . . . what else to call him. 'Not David too?'

'Nicholas,' he said reluctantly. 'But David was my second name, I have a right to use it.'

May even have given the two of them the idea of impersonation, I thought. 'You didn't take it too seriously, did you?' Ellen asked me. 'Not get it out of proportion?'

'She did,' said Crick.

Ellen grinned. 'I can't give them an alibi or anything like that, but I can give them a character reference. I'll stand up in court and say what good boys they are.'

'I'm sorry,' I said.

I said it reluctantly. Cut off from my usual professional support, I made a fool of myself and I didn't like that much.

'You're not convinced, are you?' said Crick.

'I don't know. I'm still thinking.'

Ellen Bean made her contribution, still with a grin. 'Cheer up. Good comes out of making mistakes. And you're honest. Once you look at things straight, you'll see. You'll see the truth.'

She wasn't patronizing me, just one professional talking to another.

I have had my come-uppance meted out to me once or twice in my career, some occasions being more hurtful than others. This was one of the worst.

The truth, I thought. 'Do you know it?'

187

'Of course not. I'd tell you if I knew. I do tell you what I know.'

David and Crick were both watching me with observing eyes and I saw that beneath their surface good manners and geniality, they were tough, resolute men. It wouldn't do to underrate them. I thought they could take in me and Ellen Bean with no trouble.

Just as Ellen herself seemed able to manipulate me.

I looked at the bags in the hall. 'Are you still thinking of going away?'

David looked at Crick, then answered for them both. 'Maybe.'

'Stay around,' I said. 'That's my advice.'

I walked out of the house, back to my own. I looked longingly towards the Incident Room set up in a long trailer outside the church, realizing once again how much I missed my colleagues and their support. But I had bowed out of that for this case for the time being and could not go back on it. I was used to working as part of a team, but now I was on my own.

There remained Clive Barney, but he had not been in touch again. Probably he was not as interested in me as I was in him.

Another jolt to my self-esteem. It was a pleasure to get back to my own house to meet the uncritical eyes of my cat and dog.

No messages on the newly installed answerphone, no post. Not even a newspaper.

I was the forgotten woman.

I had not realized before how much I depended on my professional life to bolster up my private persona. I had been one single person once, now I was splitting into two parts. No wonder people feared retirement: half of what they were disappeared.

I fed both animals, considered eating myself but decided that I was not hungry enough to bother. I sat there, longing for the telephone to ring or someone to bang on the door. No one did. Even the animals disappeared to their own corners once they had eaten.

It was obvious that as well as being a non-person, it was going to be a non-day. Irritatingly my ankle began to throb.

I could clean the house, I could do some cooking, I could iron a dress and shirt I had washed yesterday. I could drive into Windsor or Reading. Or even Oxford. I had friends in all three towns who would be glad to see me. I did none of these things.

I didn't want to go out into the village. The encounter with Crick and David had destroyed my pleasure in it, tearing away the superficial layer of pleasantness to reveal a smirking dislike underneath. I didn't even like my house so much now.

A very unappealing side of myself was appearing. Self-pity can only go so far and then you should give it a kick. Come back, Charmian Daniels.

Without thinking about it, I was on my feet and making my way outside to the cellar steps. Since I had last taken a look down here, and I looked at it more often than I admitted, some official hand had replaced the old seal on the door with a new one. I was annoyed, not liking what felt an invasion of my house.

I tore off the seal, to hell with it, and went in. The cellar smelt sour as if the oxygen in the air had been sucked out and replaced by something rancid.

Dried stale blood and body perhaps. I felt sickish, which something murder scenes do not usually do to me as I have seen a fair number, most with the body still *in situ*.

But that had been my business, I could put a skin between my feelings and what I saw. Now I could not, this was part of my life. I had never known Chloe Devon, I had never known Bea Armitage, but I had known Thomas Dryden and been with him when he died.

I walked in to look around. It had been tidied up. Nothing had been taken away but the cast-off kitchen objects had been lined up neatly against a wall. There were the old kettle, the griddle with a hole in it, the rusty fire extinguishers, there were two, real vintage stuff, and a box of empty bottles, they were all there.

I am sensitive to places, although this is not something that I have boasted about in the past to my male colleagues.

I stood in the middle of the cellar, trying to pick an idea, a sensation, out of the air. The foetid air made me gag. I made myself take three deep breaths. The smell seemed less bad.

An idea did come. Or rather, a question: Why had my cellar been used?

I wondered what answers Clive Barney's team were coming up with, because there ought to be one, even if it was only that the killer had whims. I could ask him, it was something we hadn't discussed. Probably we hadn't discussed anything as much as we could have done. The underground conversation between us had been going on too strongly.

I jerked round, I could hear someone outside.

A light baritone voice hailed me. 'Hello? Can I come down.'

I recognized the voice, it was Tim Abbey, the vet.

'I'm coming up.'

He was standing there in the weak sunlight, the rain having stopped, looking comfortably normal and down to earth. Contact with animals must bring out the best in you, I thought. I felt relief at seeing him. Welcome back to the normal world, Charmian Daniels.

'Saw you go down and thought I'd have a word with you.' He saw my surprised look. 'No, that's not true, I wanted to see you. How's the dog?'

'He's fine now.' I closed the cellar door behind me. I pocketed what was left of the seal.

'Oh, good.' He considered, then went on: 'I met Ellen Bean and she told me she'd wormed him, and I was a bit worried. I don't trust Ellen's remedies. I always wonder what she puts in them.'

'He seems all right. I couldn't say about the worms.'

'She likes to boast to me how much better her remedies are. She'll kill someone one day.'

'Would she do that?'

He seemed to realize what he had said and stopped. 'I didn't mean that. By accident perhaps. Not on purpose, she wouldn't.'

I wanted him to go away now, so that I could think about what he had said. Could Ellen have killed Bea Armitage?

And did it have to be by accident?

Ellen was a strong woman physically; I could see her doing all the murders and letting the ferrets help, but there was something about her, a resonance I got back from her character like the ring from a piece of fine china: she was a good person.

But good people do kill, when they feel justified . . .

Ellen Bean had been close to Bea Armitage, by her own account. If it was going to be Ellen Bean as the killer it was never going to be an easy murder to comprehend or solve. She could have gone on to kill Chloe and Thomas Dryden to hide what she had done.

It seemed fantastic but murder is never humdrum, it always has its own surprises.

'People do kill for the best of reasons, as well as the worst,' I said aloud.

Tim looked surprised.

'You put animals down for their own good.'

'That's different,' he said. 'I don't know how I got into this conversation. Want me to come to take a look at the dog?'

'I think he's fine.'

'Right. I'll be off then. Just don't let Ellen Bean give

191

you any potions. She's very heavy handed with her natural drugs. Thinks just because they come from vegetation they aren't dangerous.'

'I'll stick to Dr Harlow.'

'She's had many a brush with him for doctoring his patients.'

'She has?'

'But then everyone has a brush with him at times, he's that sort.'

'I'll remember.'

I waved him off in his jaunty white van, then returned to the sitting room. I stroked Benjy's head, who stirred in his sleep to wag his tail. He wasn't dying.

I thought again about Ellen Bean as a killer. I could conceive of her killing Bea Armitage by accident. But Bea's death from unnatural causes was at this moment pure conjecture, based on Thomas Dryden's words.

Ellen might have killed Bea out of love. Euthanasia is the euphemism commonly employed here.

Or she might have killed Bea because she owed money.

All guessing, but it was interesting, now I thought about it, that neither Crick nor David nor Ellen herself had indignantly rejected the idea that Bea had not died naturally.

It was as if they knew something or suspected it. Secret, unacknowledged, possibly unconscious.

Perhaps the whole village knew. It almost certainly knew more than I did, more than it was saying.

Ellen might kill for love, but not for money. I couldn't make a picture of her killing. Not even by accident.

I stood up and spoke to the room.

'I reject you as a killer, Ellen Bean. Not because I like you, I'm not sure I do, but you don't ring true as a murderess.'

I walked towards the window, 'I trust you, Ellen, I offer you my trust, freely and willingly. Because you speak, even if sometimes maddeningly, with an honest voice.'

I felt better after I had said that aloud. I felt even better when I saw Clive Barney getting out of his car.

'I didn't expect you. In fact, I was just thinking of phoning you.'

Today was an untidy day. He had made an effort yesterday at the Dryden house.

'I knew where you were.'

'I had a question.'

'So what were you going to ask me?'

I went over to where I kept a few bottles. 'Let me give you a drink first. Whisky?'

'Thank you.'

I handed over a glass of malt whisky. I took some white wine and soda water. 'I think it's rather that I'm going to tell you something.' I don't think he wore his tie crooked on purpose, it just happened to move sideways every day with a life of its own. 'I am coming to believe that this whole business started much earlier off than we thought.'

'Oh? How much earlier?'

'I believe Bea Armitage was the first victim.'

He sipped the whisky for a few minutes. 'Good stuff,' he said absently. 'And why do you think so?'

I told him: what Thomas Dryden had said, the missing money as a motive. How Chloe and Thomas Dryden might both have had some knowledge dangerous to the killer.

He frowned. 'It's guesswork.'

'Of course it is. But all the best answers start with a good guess.'

'I agree with that.' He sounded as if he did not agree with much else. 'And any suspects?'

'It could be Crick and David Cremorne . . . He isn't, by the way. Not a Cremorne. Bea Armitage certainly knew about their little act but they claim she thought it was a joke. They may have had money off her, though. They say not but who knows?'

'Anyone else?'

193

'Ellen Bean, she could have killed Bea but not for money. If she did it then it was for love.'

'You must tell me about that sometime,' he said.

I gave him a look that stopped him; he wouldn't joke like that again.

'There's no evidence that Mrs Armitage was murdered.'

'But if she was, and Chloe Devon and Thomas Dryden knew something about it, then that is a motive for their killing. And so far there is no other motive. Do you know of a better one?'

'I still hanker for Damiani for Devon,' he said. 'That's my good idea.'

'He's not my favourite man either, but he may not have killed anyone.'

'Reluctantly, I agree. Largely because I can't get anything on him . . . If Mrs Armitage was killed, then it was in such a way that it looked natural.'

'We shall have to find out, won't we? Mary Erskine is her next of kin. I think she would back an exhumation.'

'I don't know, it needs thinking about.'

'I would do it.'

'Yes, you would. But it's up to me.'

I was out of it, he was telling me silently, the responsibility was his. I had, in any case, fought my way to a freer and more powerful position than he now had. I was older in experience and years . . . I hoped he wasn't telling me that too.

'You've gone out of your depth in your time too.' I was thinking about the episode which had brought about the enquiry I had bowed out of. It showed a certain free spirit, I thought.

'Yes. I know what you mean. By the way. Theo Kayser is taking your place. He's a decent sort, he's been in touch. I think it may all settle itself.'

'Is that why you came here today?'

'I had some bits of news to pass on.' Then he said, awkwardly but with some determination: 'I would have come anyway.'

194

The 'I can't keep away' syndrome? Surely not.

'I wanted to talk things over with you. You have a wonderful knack of clearing my mind,' he said, clarifying that point. Oh fine, I was an intellectual stimulus then. Why did it not please me more?

'So?'

'Mostly negative, I'm afraid, but a couple of small items of interest.

'Dryden died, as we knew, from the blow to the head, but he'd been damaged about either after the blow or before. Underneath the cuts were bite marks. From a small animal. Can't be identified. Neither the cuts nor the bites were mortal.

'He bled a bit, but we can't trace his path to the church-yard back beyond the bushes and trees just beyond the church. He came that way and probably stumbled and fell about but one of the roads to Reading flanks that area. He must have come that way but we can't find any signs. Unlucky that no one saw him. So we are having a job finding out where he could have come from. No one claims any knowledge in the village, of course. Although he was well liked and I think they would help if they could.' He added thoughtfully, 'I think so. We've asked house to house.'

'He could have been dumped from a car.'

'Possible. Nothing on his clothes to indicate where he'd been but they are still working on them in the lab and something may yet turn up . . . Usual things in his pocket. He hadn't been robbed.'

'That never seemed a likely motive.'

'No, but we had to think about it.'

He added: 'The same forensic team have been handling Dryden that worked on Chloe Devon. Makes things easier for comparisons and so on. Pathologist has had a look at the bites on Dryden, they seem similar to those on Devon.'

'Be strange if they weren't.'

'Yes, we took some specimens from Dryden's face.'

195

I winced at the images evoked.

'She – a young woman, very good at her job – found traces of disinfectant on the bites . . . a common or garden sort, based on a concentrated form of iodine.'

So that was what Rewley had been talking about. He always got on to things before anyone else. Contacts like his were worth having.

'I don't know what to make of it. You don't seem surprised.'

'I am,' I said quietly. 'I'm thinking about it . . . That's one item, so what is the other?'

'It's the knife cuts . . . very free and easy, so the path man says, couldn't do better himself. Good brushwork.'

'Does he mean a professional?'

'Not necessarily, but someone adept with their hands . . . Someone with strong wrists, a good eye, and a certain nerve.'

'Any suspects?'

'We're running over the inhabitants of Brideswell with a comb,' he said. 'Doctors, vets, butchers, artists and craftsmen.'

'I suppose it is someone local?'

He groaned. 'When I said you cleared my mind, I didn't mean I wanted you to blow it wide open . . . I hope it is a local, because if not, then we shall never find who. There are no arrows pointing anywhere else.'

He had something else to say. 'I hear you've been in the Dragon asking questions.'

I didn't ask him how he knew, but he told me.

'The barman, Alf Tintern, was at school with one of my sergeants.'

'And he just happened to say?'

'That's right,' said Barney apologetically.

'He didn't give much,' I said.

'There isn't much to give. That's the trouble with Brideswell: all determined to know nothing.'

'He did see Dryden and Chloe Devon talking to each

other and picked up a bit of the conversation . . . It confirmed what I was thinking that they were both killed because of what they knew or had seen.'

I was suddenly hungry. I had been offered coffee by Crick and David, that seemed far too long ago. 'What time is it? Have you eaten? Let's go to the Dragon and get a meal.'

The Red Dragon restaurant was almost deserted except for a few late eaters. The barman gave me a friendly smile, then when he saw who I was with, he changed it to an assessing stare, and finally, when he saw us talking over our meal, he offered me a long, conspirational look that was almost a wink. 'I know what's going on,' he was saying. 'A man like me always does. Recognize the look, seen it all before.'

He had seen me here with Mary Erskine and Billy Daminai, and also with Humphrey. He could smell emotions. It was part of his job, but he enjoyed it. He was one of the biggest disseminators of gossip in the village. I had already guessed that much. The others were Mrs Beasley in the baker's shop and probably the Postmaster. But I guessed that Ellen Bean ran them a hard third.

Without a word being passed between us, we split the bill. I liked him for that. Humphrey usually made a small fuss. I could see that if I accepted the sapphire ring I would never pay another bill again.

The manager, who had been watching us through a inner glass window, was so anxious at the sight of two police officers lunching together in his hotel that I think he would have given us the lunch free.

As it was, he saw us to the door. He was anxious to let us know that business had been bad since the killings.

'You must have made something while the press and TV teams were here,' said Clive Barney without a lot of sympathy.

'They've all gone now.'

It was true. The assembled media teams had first shrunk and then disappeared altogether. Even violent death got less newsworthy after a time.

'Are you near making an arrest?'

'Evidence is coming in all the time,' said Barney.

'Ah.' The manager nodded. He knew a non-answer when he heard one. 'You didn't mind me asking? I thought you being in charge . . .' He was an Italian, not quite at ease with English officialdom.

'It's teamwork,' said Barney. 'Teamwork, you know how it is.'

As we walked away. I said: 'He didn't like that.'

'No, he wanted more. He's all right. I've checked him, which he probably knows. I thought he might have some connection with Damiani. Both Italians.'

'Goodness knows what Damiani is.'

'It's an Italian name. But there's no connection between the two men. Not to be traced. I still think Damiani is in there somehow.'

'You just don't like him.'

'Neither do you. We've already said this to each other.' He stood at the gate, watching while I got my keys out. Muff was waiting for me on the door step. 'He's got a man working there whom you helped put away for murder . . . but you know it.' He sounded mildly reproachful.

'I should have mentioned it.'

'Yes.'

A little sharpness there, I thought. A touch of the knife. I respected him for it. But I didn't say so.

'I see you've had the seal off the cellar,' he said.

'Oh, you noticed that, did you?'

'Saw it on my way in.'

'How did you know it was me?'

He didn't answer, but gave me that crooked smile. It had to be the result of a wound, I must look up his record. He'd certainly studied mine, so it was fair.

198

'What did you make of it? Did it give you any ideas?'

'I'm still thinking it over. It's a puzzle why my cellar should have been used.'

'One of the many puzzles. Let me know if you think of anything.'

He stood at the gate, and I waved to him from the door.

The rest of the day went quickly. I had a message from the builder to say the house was in order and I could move back in whenever I liked, but to bring a duster as it would need a good dust. A joker, that man. A happy conversation with Kate followed, including an invitation from Kate and Rewley to take dinner with them. The telephone had rung again and I had not answered but I listened to a message from Mary Erskine to say she would like to see me because life was difficult at the moment.

Later still, I had a short talk with Humphrey, who was still busy saving NATO, to say he was held up in Brussels. He sounded warm and friendly. He was a nice man and I did miss him.

It seemed a long day. You can always eat to pass the time but I wasn't hungry. I had eaten melon, grilled lobster, and salad at that late lunch with Barney, and nothing tempted me.

So I took Benjy for a walk. It was on this walk that I met Ellen Bean for the second time that day. She reprimanded me for my behaviour to Crick and David. 'I thought you liked them.'

'I do like them, but I don't like what they did.'

And I'm not sure I like you, I said inside myself. You may be good but you are powerful. I have restored your name to my list of suspects.

There she stood, tall, with big hands and a determined witch face, there was a slight cast in her left eye which came and went and which I took to be a sign. It was there now.

This was when she told me that the haunting in the village came from Katherine Dryden, no phantom or anything like that, just her troubled spirit stirring things up.

NINETEEN

Sleep was hard to come by after such a day. In the middle of the night I woke up and realized what Mary Erskine and I had in common: we were both clever women who had their emotional lives in a muddle. Not only clever, we were well educated and sophisticated as well. Lady Mary had the additional advantage of inherited skills from generations of women who had organized large households, important husbands and lovers. I was working class; she ought to have managed better.

I couldn't go back to sleep so I went downstairs to make some tea. The house felt cold but in the kitchen the ancient stove always burned. I wrapped myself in a blanket while I stared into the dark. Black sky outside with no early dawn. It matched my mood, I decided sourly.

Waiting for the sky to lighten, thoughts went racing round my mind. One of them was murdered, so Thomas Dryden had said. I found myself thinking about the death of Beatrice Armitage. Her name seem to present itself as the hidden victim. She had been old and sick so her death had been deemed due to the inevitable progression of old age. Dr Barlow had said so.

But if it was not a natural death then it must have appeared so. No overt sign of violence.

Poison then? Poison was the obvious answer. If it was not something Ellen Bean had handed out, then what?

Of course, doctors know their way about poisons and can give death certificates.

But my mind went back to the passage on poison that Katherine Dryden had chosen and which her husband had kept by him.

She had speculated that her brother and his family had died from a poison seeping from their refrigerator. Had the killer got to know of this and used the idea? I leaned back in the chair. I was sitting in the same room as Bea Armitage's old refrigerator but I was not ill. Muff, it was true, had been ill.

Bea had no other pieces of kitchen equipment, and what else there was, I had brought with me, and that was precious little.

The refrigerator was old enough, Heaven knows, but it seemed harmless. Some poisons were heavier than air, of course, so perhaps you had to be lower down on the floor to suffer ill effects. No, that couldn't be so unless Bea Armitage had regularly gone to sleep on the kitchen carpet. Her cat had died first, I recalled wondering if that was a pointer to anything. Perhaps Muff had gone down into the cellar and had a breath or two of poison so that she fell ill?

I looked across the room to where Muff was draped across a chair. She hadn't died, she seemed comfortable and fit. As I watched she opened her eyes, looked at me, yawned and stood up. Then she stalked across to the kitchen door, asking to be let out. Day had come.

I stood at the door smelling the soft sweet damp air. I felt light and empty, as if I hadn't slept or eaten enough for days. It seemed the time to get dressed, prepare and eat a breakfast. And to make it what my mother called a proper breakfast: porridge, bacon, toast and marmalade. Tea or coffee was optional.

I decided to skip the porridge. I might have to leave out the bacon as there was none in the refrigerator. Probably not an egg either. I had bread for toast and there might be some marmalade left, but I seemed to remember Humphrey making complaining noises about the lack of it at our last breakfast.

202

I suddenly missed him, his complaining, demanding physical presence; I thought with a mixture of sad embarrassment of the sapphire ring still in its box upstairs.

I dressed slowly and carefully, putting on a favourite tweed skirt with a silk shirt and a cashmere jacket. Old, but you wore old things in the country, that was one thing that Mary had taught me. Shoes also old but well polished. Expensive shoes, everything must have cost. Old and cheap would not do, cheap and new would be worse. You had to know the rules in the country, Mary said.

The skirtband felt loose, I had lost weight, something I usually welcomed but not today. It seemed a sign of approaching dissolution.

Change, anyway, I might be dissolving and turning into someone different.

Someone thinner, less positive, more open to love.

I wasn't sure if I liked that concept, it felt dangerous. I hadn't been too lucky in love in the past. I went over to the drawer where the ring in its box was hidden under a pile of tights. Still there, safe. How terrible if it had been stolen.

When I put it on the ring slipped easily up and down on my finger. Now that was dangerous, I might lose it, so I put it back in the box, arranged the tights over it again, and closed the drawer.

It would be a good idea to eat the breakfast I had fancied, right to the last piece of toast, and I knew where to go. I would walk across to the Red Dragon and take a meal there.

Before I left I telephoned Rewley with a question. I could have asked Clive Barney to find out, but I preferred to ask Rewley. It seemed less disloyal to Humphrey.

Rewley sounded brisk and alert early as it was. He said he'd do what he could but scientists were not really his beat.

I knew this was an excuse. 'But you knew whom to ask?'

203

'Sure, but why not do it yourself?'

He disapproved of the way I was hiding in Brideswell. Didn't like its influence on me. Or was that what Kate said?

'Let me know,' I replied, not answering his question. 'See you at your dinner party. Who else is coming?'

But he didn't answer, that was his revenge.

The Red Dragon, in the person of the head waiter, received me with polite caution. I could see he wondered what I was up to now arriving for breakfast. He looked around as if he expected me to join someone.

'On your own, Miss Daniels?'

'On my own.'

But he gave me a good table in the window where I was quickly served. The room was empty except for two middle-aged ladies who were eating while studying a road map. I heard one of them say: 'We've done Windsor and I think we ought to do Oxford before Stratford, it's kind of on the way, and I do want to see Magdalen College where C. S. Lewis taught. I'm such an admirer. I love the hobbits.' Her companion said: 'Oh, Dotty,' in a depressed tone, as if she had heard this before. 'Tolkien, Tolkien,' I heard her mutter dolefully, like the tolling of a bell.

'Bacon or kipper, miss? I can recommend the kippers. We buy them specially from the Isle of Man.'

'Bacon, please.'

Through the window I saw several couples going through the village carrying trowels and spades.

'What's that about?' I asked the waiter as he brought my coffee.

He barely looked out. 'It's the Best Kept Village week. The judges will be coming round tomorrow. Someone will probably be calling and asking why you haven't weeded out the dandelions in your front garden.'

I didn't even know if I had dandelions, but there was a fair chance that I had and more besides. At once I decided to let them stay there, determined not to be bullied into good behaviour, even with dandelions.

Somehow the richness of my breakfast seemed to be weighing me down, dragging me into a pit of self-pity. I turned towards the churchyard. It felt the natural place to go to in my present mood. The sun was shining today but it was not raising my mood.

The churchyard appeared empty at first until I saw two figures on their knees in the distance. No, not praying but weeding, which perhaps was the equivalent exercise in Brideswell today. One figure stood up to stretch which gave me the chance to recognize Ellen Bean. I had to guess that the other figure, who remained kneeling and wore a dark brown deerstalker hat, was her husband. I was not surprised to see Ellen doing her duty by the church because she had told me how hallowed this spot was, having been the site of a Roman temple and before that dedicated to a pagan earth goddess. For Ellen the goddess was the one that counted.

I did not want to speak to Ellen, so I turned away to sit in the church porch. The church door was open so that the smell all churches seem to have, of old stone and wood faintly tinged with candle wax and incense, floated out, but it was a peaceful smell. I hesitated for a moment, then went inside. I sat down in one of the old-fashioned wooden pews and closed my eyes. I didn't want to speak to either god or goddess but perhaps one of them would speak to me. A few words of advice would be welcome.

I had plenty to think about. Foremost in my mind was the idea that the murderer of Chloe Devon, Thomas Dryden, and possibly Bea Armitage would never be caught.

His or her identity might become clear to the police: the police often know the name of a killer, but proof of guilt did not always follow.

A wily, clever, slippery killer. One who acted spontaneously as the opportunity offered, always the hardest sort of killer to catch.

The great ally of the investigator, chance or luck, might not operate here.

From underneath this surface preoccupation my own personal anxieties rumbled out like an underground train coming out of a tunnel into the daylight.

I was in the awkward position of being strongly attracted to two men. Not in love, I no longer had much heart for that state of mind. I had outgrown it or it had outgrown me, couldn't be sure which. But what was happening to me might be worse. Painful, because I valued loyalty. I looked for it in my friends and colleagues.

Suddenly I wanted to walk away from both men.

Then a voice said: 'Are you all right?'

I opened my eyes. It was the rector, Thomas Baxter. Wordlessly, I stared into his gentle, concerned face.

'Yes. I'm sorry. I am fine.'

He was doubtful. 'You don't look it . . . It's Charmian Daniels, isn't it? I heard you give a talk once in Oxford on criminous women.'

'I remember that. Don't remember you.'

'We didn't speak . . . I didn't ask a question.'

'No one did. I remember thinking it was a bit like a university sermon.'

He laughed, but said: 'You are in trouble.'

'Troubled.'

'Many of us are at this time in Brideswell,' he said with some sadness. 'Can I help?'

He couldn't help, I thought. He was a scholar and churchman, too good, too gentle.

'Come into the vestry and have some coffee.'

I shook my head. 'Thank you but no. I've had too much coffee already.'

'I don't think there is anything else,' he said doubtfully. 'Except for the communion wine . . . there might be some lemonade but it may not be very nice.'

The lemonade was quite as nasty as he had predicted. He said he thought it was left over from the last Boy Scouts' meeting.

'Do you believe in ghosts?' I was watching the bubbles in the glass.

'Not in connection with murder,' he said at once.

'No, they don't kill, do they? Except by proxy.'

'Is that what you believe?'

'It's been suggested.'

'Disbelieve it,' he said, his voice stern. 'And I can guess who told you.'

'Yes.' I let the bubbles subside in the lemonade. 'I expect you can.'

He said nothing more, leaving it to me. I think the Scouts may have spiked that lemonade because I found myself talking to him, pouring it all out. The murder, my own problems. His face gave nothing away.

'You don't love either of them,' he said at the end. 'Perhaps you never can.'

Why had I thought he was soft, easy? He was diamond-hard.

He let that sink in, then said: 'And you think you know the killer but aren't sure.'

I muttered something about this person being a healer.

'My dear girl, you are an innocent. If that is the way your mind is working you will never see further into the wood.'

'What do you mean?'

He got up. 'That's all I'm saying.'

I walked back into the village, shoulders hunched, head down, reflecting on our conversation. The Rector of Brideswell was handsome and somewhat dramatic, and could handle a good bit of dialogue. I wondered if he'd ever been on the stage.

I wondered what he really knew, and if I could make him talk to me. Are there any secrets of the confessional in the Church of England? I could make a quiet threat, pointing out that people who knew who the killer was seemed to die fast themselves round here lately. I walked back to find him.

But he was nowhere to be seen. Ellen Bean and her partner had disappeared as well.

The church door was locked so I tried the rectory, a neat new bungalow, the old Queen Anne rectory having been sold years ago to a banker. No answer here either. I waited for a few minutes then went back the way I had come.

My breakfast had fuelled my energy. I began to walk fast. I had a map of the village in my head and I followed a route my mind had unconsciously prepared me for.

Everywhere in this village were geraniums and small, furry, toothed creatures. Beyond the church to the edge of the village. Up Ruddles Lane, past the Midden. I paused here for a look round, but there was no sign of anyone at home. A distant barking from the back of the house suggested that a dog had picked up my presence.

I wondered where the Beans kept their ferrets. By standing on my toes, I could see over the top of the garden wall to the roof of a long shed. The barking was closer and louder, so I moved away.

I always carry a notebook with a pen in a pocket somewhere, years of training play their part here; I pulled a page from it.

Called to see you, I wrote. *I'll be in touch.*

No overt threat there, I thought, you could read into it what you liked.

I strode on. Out of the village, up a hill and a turn down the lane called Marvell's Ride. From this lane I could see the roof of Dr Harlow's house, and more distantly on the Bennington Road where the vet had his establishment.

I walked more slowly down Marvell's Ride, which was a pretty curving road fringed with trees behind which various large houses hid themselves. It looked opulent and comfortable, making it clearly where the wealthier commuters lived. This land did not belong to the Cremorne estate.

The Harlow house could not be seen from the road so that I had to walk down a short drive. I wanted to look at it just in case Bea Armitage's money had gone that way.

The doctor had built himself a beautiful small modern house, but it was undeniably expensive. But it was also unfinished. A side wing which looked as if it had been meant to house three cars with a set of rooms above stood bleakly empty, roofed but otherwise a shell. I wondered if the stories of him having extragavant tastes was true. I thought I could believe it. A house like this cost money, money that might have run out.

A shrill burst of barking suggested that the Jack Russells were on the loose. They were dogs with sharp little teeth. Had they bitten Chloe Devon's dead body?

I must have taken too long on my survey because a figure appeared at the front door.

Not Dr Harlow but young, female, and beautiful. Also unfriendly. 'Did you want anything? We don't buy from the door.'

I ignored the attack. 'I wanted to see the doctor.'

'This is not where he consults.' She looked expensively dressed but somehow insecure of tenure. A bit of passing trade, I thought.

'Just a social call,' I said. 'Tell him Charmian Daniels called. He knows me, I live in Bea Armitage's house.'

If she had not been there I would have prowled round the back to see if I could identify anything interesting where a body might have been hidden for a time and where the dogs could have got at it. The site was very open plan, I would have found it, but I had trailed my coat enough so I gave her a smile and moved away. She stood watching me until I was on the road. I left her still watching my back. A nervous girl all right.

I had a choice now: I could continue down the lane which led I knew to the main road which I could either follow or I could strike off across the fields towards the church and the village. This was probably shorter and quicker than the way I had come. It had begun to rain so I put my head down and walked downhill.

I was intent on my walk and my thoughts; what drove a man to murder when all his training must be the other way? The training gave the knowledge of the use of poison, the handiness with the knife.

But I could be wrong: you could read about poisons and their use, and every housewife knew how to wield a knife. Was I going wrong: without my trained professional back, wasn't I just a guesser like any lay person?

I was so deep in my perplexity that I almost walked into a car.

There was a scream of brakes. 'Damn you,' said a voice. 'What do you think you are doing?'

It was Tim Abbey, driving his white van with his assistant and girlfriend Lu by his side.

I stared at him. 'Sorry.'

'So you bloody well should be. I could have killed you.'

'Steady, Timmy,' said Lu, putting her hand gently on his own scarred hand. 'Don't blow up.'

I took a deep breath. 'My fault. I was thinking. Not looking where I was going.'

'You can say that again . . .' He took a deep breath. 'Right.'

'Would you like a lift?' said his girlfriend softly.

'Thanks.' I thought she was a good girl and probably deserved all the diamonds he could give her. I climbed in and sat beside them on the long front seat in the van which smelt of chemicals and animals. Lu, however, smelt of Chanel Number 5.

'Where do you want to go?'

'Home,' I said.

As we drove past the church, we could see that a

210

protective police cordon had been put around Mrs Armitage's grave.

I needn't have gone walkies, I thought. Clive Barney was doing my work for me.

'What's going on there? said Tim.

'Gardening,' I said. 'Tidying up the churchyard.' I felt sick. The breakfast, probably.

When I got home there was a message from Rewley on the answerphone, replying to the question I had asked.

Yes, there was one other piece of kitchen equipment that could contain methyl bromide, and which could leak out lethal doses. A fire extinguisher, if old and rusty, would do it.

I went into the kitchen and put my hand on the marks on the plaster where something had hung. There had been a nail in the wall from which some object, now missing, had been suspended. There was a similar mark close by.

I went outside again, took those dangerous slippery steps down to the old cellar, on whose door the police seal had never been replaced, and in the light of a torch sought out the two rusty extinguishers. I let the torch play over them and even in that light I could see that rusty as they were the holes punched in the base and sides looked deliberate. Someone had taken care to assure there was a leak.

I telephoned Rewley, who was out, so I left message of thanks for his work and a request that he ring back.

I tried to speak to Clive Barney, but I was told he had gone to Reading in connection with an exhumation order. I knew what that meant, the whole village probably did by now: Bea Armitage.

The tangled web of deaths was beginning to unravel itself; I could sense it happening.

211

I fed the animals and let Benjy into the garden. I was glad when he came galloping back. All day I had felt brave and full of energy, but now as darkness came on, I felt very tired.

It was probably all done, but I wanted to be out of it. I could not say for sure who the killer was but I knew the group from which the killer must come.

I made some tea and I was drinking it when the telephone rang. I picked it up quickly. Let it be Clive Barney or Rewley, but it was Mary.

She sounded happy and excited. 'Darling, my soldier boy has come back and all is forgiven.'

'He didn't have much to forgive,' I said a bit sourly, I wasn't too sure where I stood on men and their rights just now.

'He thought so, but he understands now, and we're happy. I've given Billy back his ring. Thank goodness we hadn't put in it *The Times*, so no harm done. I don't think he minds too much, his mother didn't like me.'

Billy Damiani, I thought. This is where I came in.

I went up to the bedroom to pack a case. I'd go back to Maid of Honour Row in the morning. I wasn't sure what would happen about this house. I remembered that I had never found out who had made that telephone call to me advising me to cut my losses and get out, but as I thought about I decided it was Ellen Bean. Her voice made gruffer and deeper to disguise it.

Maybe she knew something that I didn't know and that this house would bring me bad luck. Or was it that she had decided I was a threat to David and Crick so I ought to be warned off? She was protective of those she loved.

She had been right on one score: a ghost had walked in Brideswell and perhaps it had been Katherine Dryden's, who might have killed herself because she missed her twin, working through the grief of her husband, making him act. Could you believe in that sort of thing?

In this mood and this place, it was hard to resist belief.

212

Then the doorbell rang, softly but insistently. I hesitated but I knew I had to go down.

A figure shrouded in a dark cloak, hood drawn down, stood there.

'Oh, you.' I had no difficulty in recognizing who it was. I suppose I had half expected this caller.

'Can I come in?'

I held the door open and Ellen Bean walked through. A wave of cold, damp air came with her.

She stood there, more aggressive than I had remembered. 'They're digging up Bea Armitage. You organized that.'

'I may have suggested it.'

'I don't know what good you think it will do. I don't hold with digging people up.'

'Neither do I, as rule.'

'You think she was poisoned?'

'I'm sure of it. I think someone she trusted gave her a hot drink or strong whisky and laced it with sedative so she slept.'

'She didn't die in her sleep.'

'No, she was sick and dizzy and went into a coma. I wasn't here, but I guess that's a good description of how she died.' Ellen Bean was quiet. 'You see I've read up what the poison she died from does to you.'

Ellen said: 'They won't discover any poison. She's been dead too long.'

'We shall have to see, won't we? Worth a look, I think.'

'You should let the dead rest,' said Ellen.

'Ah, but they won't, will they? You know that yourself. Ghosts, Ellen, didn't you say? Ghosts have teeth. From that first killing, the motive for which was money, the two others followed.'

'You put things . . . tidily.'

'I like things tidy.'

Ellen opened the door. 'I'm going. But I warn you: don't go to sleep tonight, or you might sleep too long yourself.'

She put one hand on my wrist: a real witch's grasp, strong and cold and sinewy. She could put on the cold like a garment.

'You won't get rid of me that easily, Ellen Bean,' I said. 'I am beyond your control.'

I held the door for her to depart, wondering if she would ever come back.

Darkness came early that day. I drew the curtains, put a rug round my shoulders, sitting on the bed to think. The two animals joined me.

It was Benjy who woke me with his soft, insistent growls. I sat up. I could not hear a noise but the dog was sure that someone was in the house.

I got up and crept downstairs where I stood listening. All was dark and quiet. 'No one here,' I said to Benjy. 'Go back to bed.'

The dog stood, foursquare, ears cocked and growled again. This time I did hear something and the noise was coming from under the kitchen floor.

The outside cellar.

I took my torch and went outside, the dog came with me. The garden was quiet and empty. No one around in the street and the lights out at the Red Dragon. I must have slept soundly and long.

The cellar door opened and a masked and hooded figure stood in the opening. Behind me, the dog growled. But tentatively, quietly, doubtfully, as if this was not someone you growled at.

My torch light shone on the mask, floated down over the hand, and on to the feet. There was a moment of recognition.

'I know who you are,' I said to the figure. 'And I know why you've come: it's because you know Bea Armitage is being exhumed and you've come to take away the fire extinguishers that you used to poison her with. Bea Armitage to whom you owed money.'

He grabbed me and started to drag me into the cellar. I hung on to the door frame.

'I don't know why you killed Chloe Devon, but she must have seen you on one of her trips to the village. Perhaps you were doing something puzzling with those same extinguishers when Bea Armitage died. Moving them out perhaps? Dressed up like that? What did you call yourself?'

I didn't expect an answer but after a shocked silence, I got one. 'The fire extinguisher man. She was checking on the house for a London agent on the very day when I was moving them out of the house as a precaution . . . Then she saw me again, when I gave her a lift the night she left the Dragon . . .' He stopped talking suddenly, eyeing me with those cold bright eyes I had thought so beautiful.

'You should have worn gloves,' I said. 'I recognized you by your hands and the scars on them. Chloe Devon recognized you by them and that was why you killed her.'

I looked towards Tim Abbey. Veterinary surgeon, dog lover, and woman killer. But a lover of women too, I guessed blonde Lu meant everything to him. Had he spent the money on her, breeding minks that he couldn't sell and had probably now killed, and promising her diamonds she would never get.

'I couldn't pay Bea, not without losing everything. I owed the VAT man, I'd a mortgage I couldn't afford on the clinic. We both work there. Lu loves it all. I couldn't risk losing Lu.'

Sex and money had been Baby's diagnosis, and she had been right.

'She didn't suffer, I gave her a good drink of whisky with a strong sedative in it, she liked a drop. I took one with her and then waited for her to go to sleep . . .'

'How did you know to use the extinguishers?'

'Read an article, famous case, but Kath Dryden put

215

me on to it. Told me one day when she brought the cat in. She died herself just after.'

He started to tell me the story again, but his eyes got colder and colder. I began to edge away.

'I went back to collect them in a mask and a white apron, so no one would recognize me. Chloe Devon came into the garden, she said she was on a job from the house agent. She asked me who I was and I said I was the fire extinguisher man . . . She laughed. Then when I gave her the lift from the Dragon that night, she recognized who I was and laughed again. She said it was a good story to tell at dinner . . . If only she hadn't said that . . . She was a good-looking girl, that was why I picked her up. It was how I met Lu, she was hitch-hiking to Bristol. Never got there . . . I killed Devon in the van and took her back to the barn where I kept the . . .' He hesitated. 'They got out and started on her.'

Not ferrets or Jack Russell dogs or rats, I thought, but minks, just as sharp toothed and vicious and never going to be a profitable investment or to drape the lovely Lu.

'I couldn't leave her there because of Louise always looking around, so I brought the body here one night when there was fog and rain and . . .' Again he hesitated. 'Cut her up and drove around depositing her wherever I could. Once you've killed, you see, the rest is easy.'

What a blackness behind that beautiful friendly face, I thought.

'I don't know how Dryden got interested, but he did.'

I thought we might never know that, one of the little mysteries that would never be tidied away, but I guessed it had something to do with that extract on methyl bromide that his wife had kept. As he died he had tried to tell me. 'One of them was murdered,' he had said. And dying, had tried to shape the words *fire extinguisher*.

'He came around, got into the barn, and made the creatures bite him. He wanted it for proof, he said. He was mad. Barking. I calmed him down and put disinfec-

216

tant on the bites, then I hit him on the head and tried to cut the bites away. They would have been evidence, you see . . . I thought he was dead, so I left him while I did a clinic. But he got away . . . I knew I was done for then.'

He took a step forward. 'And now I must do for you.'

He swayed. I kicked him in the groin and he screamed. As he staggered backwards, I pushed him into the cellar and closed the door.

Then I ran to the house and picked up the mobile telephone. I heard the van drive away just as I was dialling the police number.

It was a long night, which I spent in the Incident Room making a statement. The van crashed on the M4 just north of Reading; it caught fire and burnt out before anyone could get there. The traffic police said no other vehicle was involved, it was just mad driving. The motorway was closed for several hours.

It was a village murder after all. If Chloe Devon had not run away from Billy Damiani that night she would still be alive. Thomas Dryden too probably. Only Bea Armitage and her cat would have gone prematurely but perhaps Bea wouldn't have minded too much. I could imagine her saying: 'What's money? I'll manage somehow.'

But I guessed that Mary would be making a claim on the estate, although I doubted if she would get much back. And what about Lu? But girls like Lu don't go in want for long.

Clive Barney walked back to the house with me. We had said nothing to each other all the night except about the case.

'One thing of interest,' he said in a tired voice. 'It seems that Chloe Devon had been photographing documents from Damiani's office about some dicey deals . . . I think that may have been what they were really quarrelling about that night.'

217

So Baby had been right again, I conceded. Chloe was a girl who would be looking for a chance to get rich. A girl like that was looking for a death.

'And by the way, in case it worries you, and I think it did, the real reason the girl had your name and address in her pocket may have been that she admired you.'

I was surprised. 'That's hard to believe.'

'Yes, a girl she worked with said she had seen you in an interview on the local TV talking about your life and work, and she thought a career in the police might be her style.'

'She seems to have had an investigative skill all her own, but I don't think what I do would have suited her particular talents. I don't want to laugh at her, she's dead, poor girl.' But I was touched by the story.

At my gate, I stopped. 'I'm going back to Windsor tomorrow.'

'Good idea. May I telephone you?'

'Yes, please. I would like that. You know where to find me?'

'I know where to find you,' he said. 'I always know where to find you.'

He sketched a kind of salute and walked away.

I lay on my bed too tired and tense to sleep. I didn't know what lay in the future for me. Humphrey with his distinguished name and his sapphire ring or Clive Barney.

I yawned and closed my eyes. I thought I would take that chief constables course. It was an interesting idea.

In my sleep Ellen Bean was circling above my head, her black cat floating with her. 'Come back soon, Charmian Daniels,' she was saying. Wreathed about her head as in a cartoon were the words: I will tell you the real secrets of the village, about the Rector and Dr Harlow and what guilt Crick and David truly have. 'Come back, Charmian, I like a bit of devilment.'